MOTHER KNOWS BEST

A TALE OF THE OLD WITCH

MOTHER
KNOWS BEST
A TALE OF THE OLD WITCH
BY SERENA VALENTINO

DISNEP PRESS
LOS ANGELES • NEW YORK

Printed in the United States of America
First Hardcover Edition, August 2018
10 9 8 7 6 5 4 3 2
ISBN 978-1-368-00902-7
FAC-020093-18281
Library of Congress Control Number: 2016963495
This book is set in 13-point Garamond 3 LT Pro.
www.disneybooks.com

*Dedicated to Eric Russell, Sarah Cook,
Chrys Lear, Linda Seaquist-Klein, Joshua Archer,
and Darick Robertson for your unwavering love
and support over the years*

CHAPTER I

QUEEN OF
THE DEAD

Tucked snugly away deep within the dead forest lived a family of witches. Their gray cobblestone mansion was perched on the tallest hill, which looked down on a vast landscape of lifeless trees with brittle and twisted branches that resembled long grasping hands.

Around this forest was an impenetrable thicket of rosebushes with tiny beautifully preserved rosebuds still clinging to them even though they had been dead longer than anyone still living could properly recollect. This was the boundary between the land of the living and the forest of the dead, and the witches who lived in the woods rarely crossed the boundary to do harm to those living on the other side. They asked for only one thing in return: their dead.

The witches' forest wasn't merely filled with lifeless trees. It was where the dead rested—or so the neighboring villagers liked to tell themselves. They chose to think of the woods as a cemetery they weren't permitted to visit, and the witches as its caretakers, though deep within their hearts they knew their deceased loved ones were given very little peace in what should have been their eternal resting place.

But we won't concern ourselves with that part of the tale at the moment. Right now, our story centers on three sister witches—Hazel, Gothel, and Primrose—and their mother, Manea, the dreaded queen of the dead, one of the greatest and most feared witches of any age.

Manea always let it be known that her daughters were a disappointment to her, pointing out that even though the three of them were born on the same day, they were not identical. It was widely accepted in the magical realms that having identical witch daughters was a great honor. They were highly favored among the gods, because they possessed greater power and magical ability than the average witch. Though Gothel and her sisters were, by definition, triplets, they couldn't possibly have been more different from each other.

Let's start with Gothel, the youngest sister by a mere handful of hours. She possessed raven hair and dark features, with large expressive gray eyes. Her hair was thick, wild, and unruly, often filled with little bits of twigs or dried leaves from her following her sisters around in the dead woods and romping through the landscape of cemeteries within its boundaries. When Gothel chose to look up from one of her precious books long enough to notice her surroundings, she had a very large personality, demanding the attention of everyone in the room. She was a thoughtful, pragmatic young woman, rarely ruled by her emotions and singularly focused on eventually taking her mother's place in the forest of the dead. There was only one thing more important to her.

Her sisters.

Hazel, the eldest sister, was lanky and shy, with large light blue eyes. Her hair was a brilliant shade of silver, and cascaded over her shoulders like a shroud. She moved silently like a wraithlike goddess, which was fitting, really, considering where she and her sisters lived. Hazel was a soft-spoken and exceedingly empathetic young lady, always willing to listen to her sisters' problems and lend her support.

That leaves us with Primrose. Now, she was a striking redhead, with sparkling green eyes, a peaches-and-cream complexion, and a light smattering of freckles across her nose. She was lighthearted and fun, always ready for adventure, and doomed to be entirely driven by her emotions, which sometimes vexed her sisters, causing the three to quarrel.

The sisters spent much of their time in the dead woods, exploring the mausoleums and reading the names off the headstones in what felt like to the sisters a small city of the dead. They spent hours walking the various pathways of beautiful and ornate tombstones, statues, and crypts, sometimes saying the dead's names aloud as they passed them, reciting the names off the tombstones, singing them almost like a song.

With little else to fill their time, the sisters found happy occupations to keep themselves busy while traversing the dead forest. Hazel loved to bring thin pieces of delicate parchment and coal with her on their long walks in the woods so she could make impressions of some of the more ornate and decorative headstones. She called them rubbings. Sometimes she found a name on one of the headstones particularly interesting or funny and she would make a rubbing simply for reference. Later she would look up the person in her mother's large leather-bound ledger that contained the names and origins of every person buried within their woods, which made her feel less alone. Not that her sisters' friendship wasn't enough, mind you, but she liked to imagine some of the dead as her friends. She and her sisters were quite alone in the dead woods aside from their mother, who was busy and sequestered away at every opportunity, occupied with her magic, leaving little time to spend with her daughters. So Hazel found comfort and company in reading about the dead in her mother's ledger, feeling like she was getting to know the people who spent their afterlife in her forest.

Primrose often brought along her scarlet drawstring pouch, which contained a spool of ribbon, a small silver knife, and various wishes she had written on bright red parchment that she would hang from the dead branches on ribbons. It was just like Primrose to bring color into their stark world. Almost as if she had been created for the purpose of bringing beauty into their lives, because it did seem to follow her wherever she wandered. Primrose fancied the dead haunted their forest at night, reading her wishes while she and her sisters were asleep. She hoped the dead would love their afterlife. She wanted it to be a beautiful resting place rather than the dull gray landscape it really was.

Gothel was more rooted in the physical world than her sisters, with her eye always on the future.

She often brought along one of her mother's books when she went into the woods with her sisters—a book she had slipped into the pocket of her skirts when her mother wasn't paying attention. She always took the opportunity to read when her sisters stopped to do a grave rubbing or tie wishes in the trees. Sometimes she read aloud to her sisters, but usually she just let herself drift into other worlds— worlds she desperately wanted to inhabit. The world of magic. And this day was no different.

"Gothel! Move! You're blocking the headstone I want to do next!" Gothel looked up at Hazel, who gazed down at her disapprovingly. The sun was directly behind her, creating a shimmering silhouette that emphasized her ghostlike face.

"But I'm comfortable here, Hazel. Can't you rub one of the other headstones?" Gothel asked, squinting to see her sister clearly.

Hazel sighed. "I guess."

Gothel watched Hazel walk into the brilliant sunlight, which was low in the sky and cast a lovely orange-and-pink glow on their otherwise dreary landscape. It was Gothel's favorite time, the magic hour. She had read there was a land where it was eternally twilight, and she wondered what it must be like to live in such a place. "Don't go too far, Hazel!" called Gothel. "It will be dark soon, and Mother will want us home."

Hazel didn't answer her sister, but Gothel knew Hazel had heard her. Gothel had read about sister witches who could read each other's minds, and she knew that wasn't the case with her and her sisters— not quite—but they did have an understanding. At least that was what their mother had called it: "an understanding." Ever since they were very small, each had known how the others were feeling. They couldn't communicate with each other without speaking, so they didn't hear the exact words, but they did get a sense of what the others *might* be thinking from each other's emotions. Gothel had searched her mother's books for the term "understanding" and decided it must be something her mother had made up, because she couldn't find a reference to it in any of them. And she wondered if maybe someday, when they learned more of their mother's magic, she and her sisters would have the power to read each other's minds.

"What are you thinking about, Gothel?"

Gothel laughed, looking up at Primrose, who was surrounded by beautiful bright red hearts hanging in the black and twisted tree branches. Primrose had clearly been busy while Gothel had been reading her book. "You seem sad to me, Gothel. What's the matter?" asked Primrose, her brow furrowed.

"Nothing, Prim." Gothel directed her attention back to her book.

Primrose shoved her ribbon and little knife into her pouch, walked over to her sister, and sat down beside her. "Really, what's the matter?" she asked, putting her hand on her sister's.

Gothel sighed. "It's Mother. I don't understand why she won't teach us her magic. Every generation of witches in this family has shared their magic with the new generation. How are we to uphold our family's traditions if we have no idea how to do the magic?"

Primrose squeezed her sister's hand and smiled. "Because Mother never intends to die. She will always be here to honor our ancestors, so don't worry."

Gothel stood up in a huff, brushing the leaves off her rust-colored dress.

"Don't be upset, Gothel, please! Forget about Mother's magic and have fun with me and Hazel!"

Gothel was losing patience with Primrose. "But don't you see? It's our magic as well, and Mother is keeping it from us! Let's say Mother lives forever, and so do we. How will we spend our endless days?"

Primrose's green eyes sparkled in the remaining light. "We spend them exactly as we always have. Wandering these woods together. Sisters. Together. Forever." Gothel loved her sisters, but they were naive, especially Primrose. They were perfectly content to live their lives in the forest, letting their mother do her magic, having no idea how it worked. Primrose probably thought the villagers were content to give them their dead. Gothel was always keenly aware this was a topic she shouldn't bring up with her sisters, for fear she would upset their blissful ignorance and disrupt their sisterly balance.

"I love spending my days with you, Prim, I do! But don't you want to see the world outside of this forest? Don't you want to live a life of your own?"

"We *are* living a life of our own, Gothel! Don't be weird!" said Primrose as Hazel walked up the path to join her sisters.

"I can't believe you would want to leave us!" said Hazel, overhearing her sisters' conversation.

"I don't want to leave you! I want us to always be together. I couldn't live without you, but if Mother refuses to show us her magic, then I want to be with you on the other side of that thicket! I want to see the world with you." She sighed again and continued talking. "If Mother won't teach me her magic, I want to find a witch willing to teach me theirs. We're witches and we have no idea how to use our powers. Doesn't that bother you?"

"Shhh!" Hazel put her finger against her lips, cautioning her sisters to be quiet, annoying Gothel.

"Mother isn't here! You're so paranoid, Hazel!" But the sisters heard the snap of a twig, which rang out louder than thunder in the quiet woods. "Shhh! What is it?"

The sisters stood frozen in fear. Nothing lived in the forest except the witches. It was either their mother or the dead, and they couldn't decide which was more frightening. "If Mother heard you, she is going to be furious, Gothel!" whispered Hazel.

"Shhh! I don't think it's her! Maybe someone from the other side made their way through the boundary!" whispered Primrose.

"That's impossible. No one has wandered into our woods in our lifetime. Not once!" said Gothel.

"Not that Mother has told us about," Primrose said, making Gothel scoff.

"Even if a villager were brave enough to enter our woods, they couldn't get in if they tried. The thicket is enchanted. No one living can enter these woods if they're not a witch of our blood. You know how it works, Prim! I've told you this story count-less times!" Gothel thought about those words and continued, "But I suppose we really don't know how it works, do we?"

"Why are you so weird all the time, Gothel? What are you talking about?" asked Primrose.

"I'm talking about Mother! She tells us nothing! The only reason I know any of this is because I've been reading her books!"

"That's because Mother knows best."

Their mother's voice was like a knife in Gothel's stomach. She felt queasy and slightly faint at the sound of it, her knees buckling under her. Primrose caught Gothel by the arm, steadying her.

"Mother! Leave Gothel alone!" shouted Primrose, putting herself between her mother and her sister.

Manea laughed at her daughters. "This isn't my doing, Primrose. Gothel has worked herself up into a tizzy as usual. Hurting her would be like hurting myself, and I would never dream of hurting myself."

Manea stood perfectly still, staring at her daughters. Her long straight black hair hung around her, creating shadows in the hollows of her disturbingly thin face, making her visage look like a skull brought to life. Her eyes were extremely large and bulged from their deeply set sockets with rage, sending fear into her daughters' hearts.

"Please do calm down, Daughters. I'm not here to punish Gothel. You don't think I hear your every thought and know your every movement? I've known for years Gothel has been reading my books. And what do I care? That's what they're there for, to read!" She laughed again. "Clever Gothel. Secretive, blackhearted Gothel. All this time slipping books into your pockets and spiriting them away to the forest to read in secret!" Her voice held a mixture of scorn and amusement.

Manea pushed her hair out of her wrathful face with her long spindly fingers, making her look even more severe. The sister witches knew she was about to do her magic, because on the rare occasions she did her magic in front of them, she made this gesture when she was about to perform a spell.

"You want to see my magic, Gothel? You want to see what my mother taught me? You want to learn my magic? Behold!"

Manea raised her hands skyward, illuminating

the dark forest with silver lightning blasts that sparked from her fingertips and crashed into the tree branches, catching them ablaze. Primrose screamed, pulling her sisters closer to her. "Mother, no!"

"I call upon the old gods and the new, bring life into these woods and give us our due!" Manea bellowed as she sent more lightning into the sky, causing a thunderous storm to erupt overhead.

"Mother, stop! What are you doing? We know you're powerful. I'm sorry I said those things about you. I'm sorry!" Gothel pleaded with her mother, but Manea just laughed as she created a tempest of swirling golden light that mingled with the storm and showered down around them.

"I call upon the old gods and the new, bring life into these woods and give us our due!"

As the golden light fell with the rain and penetrated the soil, it woke the souls that inhabited the city of the dead, inviting them to come out of their crypts and rise from under the earth. Most of them were skeletal creatures, exhausted and angry about being awoken from their slumber, while others were still in possession of their rotting muscles and putrid skin. Gothel observed the looks of disgust on her sisters' faces when they saw the creatures with dangling or missing limbs silently making their way to Manea. She felt powerful seeing these creatures, realizing that one day they would belong to her and be subject to her whims.

"I'm sorry to disturb you, my dears," said Manea to her creatures. "But I need you. One of our nearby villages are hoarding their dead. Go forth and bring them all to me."

Hazel and Primrose gasped in fear, but Gothel stood in awe of her mother's majesty. She had never seen her mother command her creatures, and it sent chills throughout her body. She couldn't fathom any of the nearby villages having the audacity to hoard their dead. For centuries, the dead had been sent to the witches. Sure, there had been times when a local villager had caused an insurrection and tried to defy the witches, but it had always been met with such violence that Gothel was sure it would never be attempted in her lifetime. Gothel could see one tall grotesque creature considering her mother's words with intense concentration.

"Leave no one alive but their children and one adult woman. Bind her to the old promise. She must tell the story of this night to future generations and warn them never to hoard their dead again!"

"Yes, my queen," said the exceedingly tall creature with leathery skin stretched over his skeletal face.

"Knock on every crypt as you go and wake all of my children. Even the young. Take them with you and show them the way. Show them how to make the living suffer for hoarding their dead."

"As you wish, my queen," said the creature. The other creatures just stood at attention, waiting for their orders, waiting for the queen of the dead to do her magic, waiting to bring the living into their ranks. The only creature who spoke was the grotesquerie who had once been a very tall man, who wore a black top hat, a long black coat, and trousers that were now tattered and crumbling like dust. The creature looked down at his own hands, examining them, his face strained as if he was surprised there was so little left of him since the last time he had been awakened from his slumber.

"You look beautiful, my love," said Manea. "Handsome as ever. I still see the man you once were. Do you see him in my mind? Hold that image as you lead this army in my name. Know that I love you and will be waiting for you to return." As she was about to dismiss her most favored minion, she remembered one last detail. "Oh, and, my love, bring the newly dead to me so we can record their names."

"Yes, my queen. And should the woman refuse the terms?"

"Then kill her and the children, my love. And bring them all to me."

"Yes, my queen."

Primrose's and Hazel's screams rang in Gothel's ears. She couldn't tell one voice from the other as they pleaded with their mother to stop.

Manea didn't seem to hear her daughters, and if she did, she didn't care. Her gaze was fixed on the thicket as she reached forward, grasping at the air with her clawlike hand and then tightening her grip as if choking an invisible victim. Then, quickly, with a flick of her wrist, she released a scarlet ball, which shot through the air and turned into a spiraling vortex, creating a pathway for her loathsome minions to cross the boundary into the land of the living. The sisters had never seen her use her magic in this way, and it made them tremble in fear.

"Go now, my love! Teach the living what it means to hoard their dead! Make them fear me like their ancestors did before them. Make it brutal and make it bloody! Fill their minds with terrors that will live on in their imaginations. Create a fear so great within their hearts they will never forget what it means to cross the witches of the dead woods!"

"Mother, no!"

Gothel was awestruck and her sisters stood frozen with fear, watching the dead march through the crimson vortex. But even more disturbing was the twisted smile on their mother's face. They had never seen her so happy, so pleased with herself, and they shuddered to think what those monsters would do to the villagers.

"Mother! Please don't do this! Can't you just give them a warning? Give them a chance to make it right before you do this?" begged Primrose.

Manea laughed at her. "You're pathetic! If you girls want to learn *my magic*, if you want to honor the ancestors, then *this* will be one of your responsibilities. Do you think I do this lightly, Prim? Do you think I take pleasure in having women and children slaughtered? I do it for our protection. For our family!"

Primrose had a look of utter disgust on her face. "I think you do take pleasure in it, Mother! *I can feel it!* So don't pretend otherwise!"

Manea narrowed her eyes at her daughter. "One day it will be up to you girls to take up this responsibility after me. It's a grave undertaking, it takes courage and resolve, and I fear you are too weak to take my place when the time comes!"

Primrose stood stark still, clinging to Hazel. It was Gothel who spoke. She took a deep breath, raised her chin to meet her mother's gaze, and said, "I choose to honor you and those who came before you, Mother. I want to learn your magic. I will take on the responsibility."

Manea grabbed Gothel by the throat, lifting her off the ground. Gothel's feet were dangling like a rag doll's as her sisters' screams rang in her ears. "What makes you worthy, Gothel, to stand in my place and rule as queen in this land?"

"I don't know," said Gothel, trembling and gasping for air. She knew she was worthy. She felt there was something of her mother inside her, waiting to get out. She knew this was her rightful place, but she couldn't put it into words.

"What would you do in my place? What would you do if a nearby village was hoarding their dead?" asked her mother, meeting Gothel's gaze.

"I would do the same as you, Mother," said Gothel.

"Good. I always hoped you would take my place here once I chose to fall into the mists, Gothel," said Manea as she gently let go of Gothel's neck.

"But that time is not now, my darling." She stroked her daughter's hair. "My magic doesn't live in those books you've been reading, not entirely. It lives in my blood, and I can spare only so much at a time." Gothel's eyes were wide as she listened to her mother, and she knew her mother could hear her thoughts and questions. "Yes, my dear one, my Gothel, you understand me now. I'm not being selfish with my powers. Once I have given you everything there is to know, there will be nothing left of me. You will have it all, including my life and my place as queen, and the responsibility to honor our ancestors will be yours. That is paramount, Gothel, that you uphold our traditions and keep our secrets safe from the world of the living." Manea looked into her daughter's eyes. "Are you ready to receive more of my blood, Daughter? To take the next step?"

"More of your blood?"

Manea laughed. "Yes, my blackhearted child, more. How do you think you and your sisters can feel each other's emotions? How do you think Primrose felt mine? That's my blood running through your veins. I shared a small amount of my blood with each of you when you were born, and I intend to share it again. The more I share with you, the more powerful you will become. Are you prepared to receive more, my daughter?"

"Gothel, no! Don't do it!" whispered Primrose. Gothel wanted nothing more than to quell her sisters' fears, to make them understand she was doing this for them, but she didn't have the words to comfort either of them. Hazel's blue eyes were filled with tears, and Primrose was shaking her head frantically as Gothel considered her mother's proposal. "Gothel, please don't!"

Manea laughed. "You two were always weakminded. So pure. Not like witches at all. Not like Gothel here. Her heart is almost as black as mine."

"Don't say that!" screamed Hazel. "If you're so sure about Gothel, then let her take the night to think it over. Give her the night to decide."

Manea laughed again. "Fine. Go back to the house, the lot of you! Gothel can give me her decision before the sun sets tomorrow. Now leave before I change my mind!"

"Come on, Gothel," said Primrose, pulling her sister away from her mother, but Gothel couldn't seem to make her limbs move. She felt numb, like she was in a trance and somehow tethered to her mother. Gothel's sisters each took one of her hands and led her down the path that would take them to their house on the hill, leaving their mother alone in the dead forest to do her magic, which erupted around her like lightning, casting terrible shadows about. With each step, Gothel had to will her legs to move. It was as if some invisible force wanted her to stay with her mother.

"Don't look back at her, Gothel!" whispered Hazel. "Focus on us." Gothel blinked, trying to focus on her sisters. She felt like she was coming out of a thick fog as they moved farther away from their mother.

"Are you okay?" asked Primrose, looking into her sister's eyes. They reflected the light from their mother's magic, which sparked in the distance, making her eyes look as if they didn't completely belong to her. "Gothel?" Primrose stopped walking, put her hands on Gothel's shoulders, and looked into her large light eyes. "Gothel! Look at me! Are you okay?"

"Yes, Prim, I'm fine. Let's go home. I have a lot to think about."

CHAPTER II

THE WITCHES ON
THE HILL

The three sisters stood on the balcony off Gothel's bedroom, watching the lights from their mother's magic dance in the dead forest. They created ominous shadows on stone carvings of harpies on the wall behind them, giving the winged beauties life.

"How long do you think she will be out there?" asked Hazel. Her voice was quivering.

"Don't be frightened, Hazel. Everything will be okay, I promise," said Gothel with a strange faraway look in her eye.

"How can you say that? Everything will not

be okay! Our mother is killing everyone in that village!" Primrose was shaking with anger.

"Our mother is upholding our family's traditions, Prim. This is the way it's been done for centuries."

Primrose looked at Gothel like she was something vile, like she was an alien species she didn't recognize.

"Don't look at me like that!" Gothel was hurt. She felt her sister's revulsion, but there was nothing she could say to make her sister comprehend why Gothel understood what her mother was doing. And no way to explain why Gothel would do the same thing in her mother's place.

"What's gotten into you, Gothel? How are you okay with any of this?"

Gothel couldn't answer.

But Primrose thought she knew. She could feel Gothel's emotions, which were swirling around inside her like a tempest of anticipation. "You want Mother's power!" Primrose exclaimed. "Don't you?"

Gothel considered it for a moment and said,

"Yes, that's part of it. But I'm not being selfish, Prim. I want her power so I can protect you and Hazel! Mother won't be here forever, and someone has to keep us safe here. What if something happens to her? What if the villagers revolt and attack us? How would I be able to protect you without Mother's magic?"

Primrose stood her ground. "Earlier you said you wanted to see the world outside the thicket, Gothel. You said you didn't want to be trapped here forever, and now you're considering taking on a responsibility that will have you tethered here your entire lifetime!" Primrose seemed to be looking into Gothel's soul, considering an aspect she hadn't seen in her sister before. "Something within you has changed! Is it because Mother said she will finally share her magic with you? Do you really believe her?"

Gothel wished her sister understood why she wanted to do this. "Of course I believe her! She's our mother!"

Primrose scoffed. "What the Hades is wrong with you? She's having everyone in that village killed! Are you actually telling me that doesn't bother you? In what universe is that not insane?"

Quite a few, actually, Gothel thought. She didn't want to upset her sister with the truth, but really there was no way of avoiding it. "It's always been done this way, Prim. Always. Long before Mother, and long before Grandmother! Mother just hasn't had to do it in our lifetime, and she probably won't have to do it again for another hundred years. I'm sure the villagers will learn their lesson and stick to the pact their ancestors made with our ancestors." Gothel paused, then continued. "And if they don't, we'll be forced to do it again until they learn. We have to make it clear we won't allow them to break the pact, that we aren't weak and we can't be taken advantage of." Gothel could tell Primrose was getting angrier with every word Gothel spoke, but she continued. "Tonight will work in our favor, Prim. Some of our horde is starting to crumble, our ranks are thinning. We could use more dead should we ever need them again."

Primrose was thunderstruck by Gothel's words.

"Need them again? To do what? Kill innocent people because they don't want to give us their dead? Oh, that's right, I'm talking to Gothel! Always the logical one! The pragmatic sister! The smartest in the lot! Well, you don't sound intelligent, Gothel! You sound like a sociopath! You sound like Mother!"

Gothel gave her sister a sad smile. "Prim, read our history! This is how it's always been, for more generations than you can fathom!"

"So what if our great-great-great-grandmothers were killing innocent people! That doesn't mean we have to! We can leave here, we can refuse! This doesn't have to be our life, Gothel! Please, let's just go the way we talked about earlier today. We can leave Mother here to do what she wishes, but I don't want any part of it!"

"We can't go, Prim. Not now. We have to stay! Hazel, tell her we can't go!" said Gothel to the silent Hazel, who was standing at her side.

"Gothel, are you really going to do this? Please tell me you're not really going to do this!" Primrose pleaded while Hazel watched her sisters argue, as

30

she often did, waiting to find the proper moment to share her feelings.

"I am, Prim, and when Mother offers me her blood, I want you and Hazel to take it with me."

"Are you insane?"

"Clearly you think I am! But I think if we all take Mother's blood tomorrow, we'll be able to share our thoughts. Think about it, Prim, I will always know if either of you need me! We will be able to protect each other."

Primrose wrinkled up her face in disgust again. "You mean you want to control us, the way Mother is controlling you now!" she spat, hurting Gothel's feelings.

"No! That's not it at all! Also, she's not controlling me!"

"Then what was that all about earlier, then? You looked bewitched!"

"I was just dizzy! I was overwhelmed by what Mother is offering us, and what all of this really means."

"You mean what Mother was offering *you*!

You've always been her favorite, and you can lie to yourself about what that means, but you can't hide your heart from me! Listen to me, Gothel, if you do this, if you take Mother's blood, I will never forgive you. I will leave this place forever and you will never see me again, do you understand?" Primrose was in tears, but she looked entirely serious.

"Prim! I love you, I love you so much! But you don't understand what you're saying! We have no idea how old Mother really is. She won't be with us forever!"

"She can live as long as she wants! She doesn't have to die if she doesn't want to! You heard her, it would be her choice to go into the mists!" said Primrose.

"What if something happens to her before she's ready to move on? How would I heal her without knowing her magic? Besides, you know one day she will be too tired to stay in this world. She will want to move on just like her mother before her, and her mother before her, and like every other witch of our blood before them. It's our duty to take her place, to make sure our family's magic lives on after she passes into the mists. We have to stay here and protect our forest and uphold our traditions. You've always known this!"

Primrose shook her head. "Not this way, Gothel! I won't be part of killing innocent people! I will never be okay with killing children! And I will never forgive you if you do this!"

Gothel felt as if her heart was being ripped out. Her mother had finally agreed to share her magic with her, and her sister was forcing her to make an impossible choice. She sighed and said, "You know you mean more to me than Mother's magic! Please don't make me choose!"

Primrose said nothing. She just stared at her sister with tears sliding down her face.

Gothel tightened her fists, squeezing them so hard her nails were piercing her palms, making them bleed. "Fine. I won't do it! You know I can't lose you, Prim! I can't! If you really don't want me to do this, then I won't. We can leave here together tomorrow before the sun sets if that's really what you want. But I want you to understand what that decision means."

Hazel, who had been quietly listening to her sisters argue, finally spoke. "No one is leaving!"

Gothel and Primrose stared at their sister in astonishment. Quiet, contemplative Hazel was taking on a role she rarely played, but it was nevertheless her place. She was the eldest sister, and her younger sisters stood there, mesmerized by how calmly and resolutely she spoke. "I will share the blood with you tomorrow, Gothel. Our place is here. We are the daughters of Manea, and we have a responsibility to the dead woods, and to our ancestors. Primrose, you know this! You've known it your entire lifetime. I don't understand why you're acting as if you've just learned about this now! Mother has always told us the stories of times before we were born. Did you think it was all fairy tales? We live in the dead woods, Prim! *The dead woods!* This shouldn't be such a shock to you! We have walked among the dead our entire lifetimes! We have heard the stories of our ancestors at bedtime since we were small. If we leave this place, there will be no one left to control the dead after Mother is gone! Do you realize what that means, Prim? Listen to me! We're *all* going to take Mother's blood tomorrow. All of us! I'm the eldest after Mother, and my decision is final."

"I can't believe you're taking Gothel's side, Hazel! You both make me sick!" Primrose stormed off, leaving Hazel and Gothel on the balcony.

"Prim, please stay! Come back!" Gothel was heartbroken. She felt she had somehow ruined everything. And she wondered if she would ever have Primrose's love again.

"Don't worry, Gothel. I think she'll feel differently tomorrow. She just needs time to think it over. You know how she is. Her anger burns bright but it also dies quickly. You know she can't stay mad at either of us for very long." Gothel knew Hazel was right, but there was something inside her that told her she might have lost Primrose for good.

"Thank you for supporting me, Hazel. Thank you for trusting me. I knew you would understand why I am doing this."

Hazel seemed to be thinking it over before responding. Finally, she said, "I think I understand. We have to do it because it's our obligation."

"It's our obligation and birthright! I've spent so many years upset with Mother because I thought she was selfishly keeping her magic from us. I was ready to leave this place for fear of languishing here forever with nothing to do but wander these woods, but don't you see? If she wants to share her blood with me now, that means she is getting ready to go into the mists. It means she is ready to move on and wants us to have her knowledge before she goes."

"Gothel, are you doing this to protect us, like you said, or are you doing it for the power?"

Gothel watched her sister walk out of the room before responding quietly, "Oh, Hazel, what would you think of me if I said I was doing it for both reasons?"

CHAPTER III

TOGETHER FOREVER

Gothel's room was filled with the hazy grayish-blue light that always accompanied sunrise in the dead woods. Gothel pulled her red velvet duvet up around her chin, feeling a slight chill. She was reluctant to greet the day and face her sister Primrose, but when she focused and really looked about, she realized she probably shouldn't be so worried. Her room was filled with red paper hearts, hung from the four posts of her bed and strung from the beams on her ceiling. She reached up and pulled one of the hearts from her four-poster and read it aloud.

"'Together forever.'" Gothel sighed, hoping it meant her sister wasn't angry with her anymore.

She stood in her room, just looking at the gray stone walls and the magnificent view of the woods from her window, realizing how much she really loved that house. For all her talk of leaving the dead woods, she realized in that moment she didn't really want to. She loved her home, even if it was cold and drafty and made of dreary cobblestone. Even if it was barren and uninspiring and covered in monstrous carvings of night creatures. It was her home, and it was where she had lived her entire life. She wouldn't know how to live in the outside world. What she had always wanted was to learn her mother's magic and to live forever with her sisters. And now it seemed her dream would finally come true. But if Primrose was going to make Gothel choose between her and Mother's magic, then the choice was simple. She would pick her sisters. And if her mother disowned her for changing her mind, then she would leave with her sisters and learn how to live in the world without magic.

As long as she had her sisters with her, she would be happy.

Sisters. Together. Forever.

There was a light knock at the door.

"Come in!" called Gothel.

It was Primrose. She was already dressed in her finest green gown, and she was holding a tarnished silver tray with two cups of tea and a pile of blueberry scones on it. "Thank you for the wishes, Prim. I love them," said Gothel, smiling at her sister.

"I have hazelnut tea, your favorite," said Primrose, smiling back at Gothel and setting the tray on the little round table beside the bed.

"Thank you," said Gothel.

Primrose sat on Gothel's bed, patting it with her small hand. "Gothel, please sit with me. I've thought about it, and I've decided I'm going to take Mother's blood with you and Hazel."

Gothel's eyes grew wide. "Really?"

"Yes. Someone will have to keep you in check, Gothel, and it might as well be me."

Gothel wrapped her arms around her sister. "Are you sure? Are you really sure? Because this is a big deal, Prim!"

"I know. But you and Hazel were right, of course. I've always known the stories. Ever since we were little, we've known who our mother is. But I think somehow, oh, I don't know, I think I managed to turn it into some sort of . . ."

"Fairy tale?"

"Yes."

"I understand."

"I've never seen Mother use her magic like that before. Somehow, I was able to tell myself the stories, and our history, weren't real."

"I understand, Prim. But can I say I think I'm worried about her? Something within her has changed. Something isn't quite right."

"I wish you and Hazel wouldn't fret over Mother so much, Gothel. She will be with us for at least another hundred years."

"I hope so. It could take that long to teach us everything she knows."

Primrose stood up from the bed, went to Gothel's closet, and pulled out a dark burgundy velvet dress and a black velvet cloak. "Here! I think you should wear this! Hazel is wearing her silver. You won't want to be the only sister who isn't dressed for the occasion."

"What occasion is that?"

"Mother's ceremony, silly! I've already told her we are all taking the blood this evening at sunset. She's in the conservatory now, making preparations!"

"Do you think she will actually let us in there?"

"Maybe . . . in another fifty years!" said Primrose, laughing. "You know how Mother is. Do you have any idea what's in there?"

"I think it's rapunzel."

"Who?"

"It's a flower. The only thing that grows in these woods lives in that conservatory."

"How do you know all of this?" asked Primrose.

"I've been reading Mother's journals for years. The flower has been in our family for generations. It will be part of our responsibility to keep it alive after Mother is gone."

"You're so weird, Gothel."

Gothel flinched. "Weird? Why?"

"Nothing! Never mind. I love you."

"Are you sure you want to do this? You're not just doing it for me, are you?" asked Gothel, afraid Primrose would change her mind.

"Stop worrying, Gothel. I'm doing this so we can always be together. Just make me one promise: when you're queen of the dead, you won't ever kill the children of the villagers."

"I promise."

"Together forever, right?"

"Together forever."

CHAPTER IV

CONTEMPLATING ANGELS

The stone path leading to the conservatory where Gothel's mother spent most of her time was flanked with dead weeping willows that quivered in the wind, making eerie patterns of light on the pathway. Gothel walked alone, taking in her surroundings. She loved the statues of weeping angels along the path, some of them peeking from behind the trees, others so old they were crumbling, with their faces chipped away by time. There was one Gothel loved most. Her favorite angel. She was made of black marble and covered in dried moss. The angel's face was covered with her hands. Gothel imagined the angel was weeping for all the dead that slumbered in their woods. Crying for an eternity. And somehow that made Gothel feel better. She wouldn't ever need to cry for the dead; the angel would cry for her.

The angel would cry forever.

Gothel wondered how many women before her had walked the path to the conservatory, contemplating the angels. She wasn't entirely sure why she was going to the conservatory other than she knew her mother was there and some inexplicable force was leading Gothel to her mother.

The conservatory was a beautiful building constructed of paned glass, like a giant greenhouse but architecturally much more stunning. It was a large structure that could be seen from the mansion, resembling a glittering jewel in the otherwise stark landscape. As Gothel got closer to the conservatory, she wondered what she was doing there. She had never bothered her mother while she was doing her magic, not once. She'd never even asked to be let in the conservatory, but she felt different that day; somehow, she felt more powerful and brave knowing later she would be gaining some of her mother's powers. Something about that day was different.

"Something about today *is* different, my pet," said her mother, standing in the doorway of the conservatory.

"Mother! I didn't see you standing there."

"Would you like to come inside, Gothel?"

"Umm . . . sure," said Gothel, walking tentatively to join her mother.

"Don't be nervous, my sweet. One day this will be your place of power." She smiled at Gothel, reached out her hand, and said, "Come inside."

The building was filled with a blinding golden light, brighter than the sun, brighter than anything Gothel had ever seen. She wondered how she hadn't seen the light from outside the building.

"Magic, my dear!" said Manea with a laugh.

Gothel was dazzled by the brilliance of the flowers, too awestruck to reply to her mother. She couldn't guess how many flowers were in the room. Her mother had placed them around the circumference of the conservatory on many rows of tiered benches, resembling seats in an amphitheater. The entire room was filled with the flowers, except the very center, which had some magical markings painted on the floor and a small wooden table with some of her mother's magical items on it.

The light of the rapunzel flowers was glowing more brightly than the lights coming from the numerous lanterns her mother had hung on large wrought-iron hooks around the room. The sight of it almost took her breath away.

"This is your real inheritance, Gothel. This is our legacy," said Manea, her arms outstretched.

"The rapunzel?" asked Gothel in a small voice.

"Yes, my intelligent beast. After I'm gone, it will be your job to protect it! This is paramount, my blackhearted child. If you intend to live as many lifetimes as I have, then you will have to protect the rapunzel, if for no other reason than to ensure you and your sisters will always be safe from the indignity of old age."

"I understand."

"I think you do, my dear." Manea paused, then

continued. "There's something I want to tell you, something you can't share with your sisters. They wouldn't understand. Remember when I said that hurting you would be like hurting myself?"

"I do."

"Did you wonder what I meant by that?"

Gothel looked into her mother's eyes, searching for the answer, and then she realized she had always known. She had felt it since she was very young, but never had the proper words until that moment.

"Because I am you. I don't know how, but I can feel it."

"You've always been the smart one, my sweet. Always so sensible. You know I love your sisters, but you're truly mine, Gothel. You're my favorite," said Manea, giving her daughter a rare smile.

"Really? Is that true?" asked Gothel, wondering if her mother was being honest with her.

"What makes you doubt it?"

"Our names," said Gothel in a small voice.

Manea laughed. "Because you don't have a flower name? You think that makes you any less precious to me? It makes you unique, Gothel. It makes you special. Now go. I have much to prepare before our ceremony later tonight."

"Mother, you're not planning to go into the mists anytime soon, are you?"

"No, dear. I have a lot to teach you before I do. Does that disappoint you?"

"No. Not at all!"

"Good! Now go! I have a lot of work to do."

CHAPTER V

BEFORE THE STORM

Gothel was quietly reading a book in the library while her sisters sat nearby, fidgeting nervously. There was a large fire blazing in the stone fireplace flanked by enormous skull statues that supported the stone mantel. The light from the flames was dancing on the numerous leather-bound books that filled the wall-to-wall bookshelves dominating the room. That was Gothel's favorite place in the world; she always felt at peace there. So many books to read and worlds to escape into, so much history to learn. No matter what was happening, no matter how distressing it was, all she had to do was go to the library and all would be well in her world. That evening was different. She couldn't distract herself from what was happening in just a few short hours. That night everything was going to change.

"You're nervous," said Primrose, curled up in a black leather chair across the room. Gothel thought it was interesting that Primrose always chose that chair: the one with the carving of an old tree filled with ravens on the wall behind it. There were many carvings like that around their mansion, but that tree was a little different from all the others; there were blooms, almost too small to see, just little sprouts, bursting from the branches, and Gothel wondered if her sister had even noticed. It was so like Primrose to be surrounded by life, and by color. She wondered how her poor sister had found herself in such a dreary place. It was as if she had been brought there from another world. Now, her sister Hazel looked like she belonged there. She looked as though all the color had been leached from her. She looked like a ghost, sitting in her chair near the fireplace, the light dancing off the carvings of winged griffons behind her.

"Am I nervous?" asked Gothel, surprised.

"Well, I know I am!" said Primrose.

"Honestly, I'm not sure how I'm feeling. Excited, maybe? I don't know." Gothel stood up. "Oh, my goodness! Think about it, Prim! In a few hours, after we take Mother's blood, we're going to be able to hear each other's thoughts, like all the time!"

"Yeah, I don't think I'm as excited about that as you are, Gothel," said Primrose, rolling her eyes.

"Why?" asked Gothel.

"Oh, I don't know, Gothel, maybe it has something to do with never having privacy *ever again*!"

Hazel interjected. "Primrose, you won't have to share what you're thinking all the time. It would be maddening to hear each other's thoughts constantly." Hazel glanced at Gothel, who was giving her a look like she was surprised Hazel knew what she was talking about. "You're not the only one who reads Mother's books, you know, Gothel."

Gothel smiled. "How should we spend our last moments as our current selves?"

"Gothel, you're so weird! Seriously, what are you talking about?" asked Primrose.

"Our lives are going to change forever today, Prim!" said Gothel. She seemed almost giddy, and it was annoying Primrose.

"That's true," said Primrose with an odd look on her face that her sisters couldn't quite read.

"What's wrong? What's that face you're making? Did you change your mind?" asked Gothel.

"She didn't change her mind, Gothel. Calm down," said Hazel. She turned to Primrose. "And you stop teasing Gothel! She isn't weird. She's right. We will be different people after tonight. Different versions of ourselves. It's not a strange question. How should we spend our last evening together before we start our schooling with Mother?"

"I don't know about you two, but I'm going to spend it alone!" said Primrose, standing up in a huff and storming out of the room.

"Primrose! What's wrong?" called Gothel as Primrose slammed the door behind her. "What just happened? What did I say?" Gothel was confused and hurt.

Hazel shook her head. "You didn't say anything.

Prim is just being her dramatic self. Her life isn't going the way she planned and she's sulking."

"What do you mean?"

Hazel smiled at her sister. "You know Primrose. She just wants to have fun. She'd be content to spend the rest of our days wandering the woods and hanging her hearts in the trees as long as she has us, and that's all changing. We're going to be spending all our time with Mother, learning how to take her place. It won't be the three of us together the way she imagined, and that frightens her. I think she already misses us."

"But we're here! We're all here! And when we take Mother's blood, we will all be more powerful. We will be able to do magic, not just feel each other's emotions. We will be able to do real magic!" said Gothel.

"I know and I'm really excited about it. But I think Primrose agreed to do this only because she knows how important it is to both of us."

"Is it really important to you?"

"It is, Gothel! I see us many years from now,

witches together learning our craft, studying into the night, practicing our spells, maybe even meeting other witches, but that isn't Primrose's sort of thing. She's afraid of how all of this is going to change our relationships. She's afraid of losing us to magic."

"But she can join us!"

"It isn't her thing, Gothel. I think we should consider letting her leave the dead woods."

"No!"

"Gothel, you realize she will leave eventually. If she stays here, she will be living the life you dreaded. Languishing forever with nothing to do! That's exactly what you were afraid your life would become. Do you want that for her?"

"But she does have something to do! She can learn magic with us!"

"Gothel! Stop. Listen to me. She doesn't want to do magic. She's afraid of it! I think she needs to be in the real world. I can feel it. I know she doesn't see herself here forever." Hazel sighed. "Gothel, do you remember when we were small, how we would all run around the city of the dead, knocking on the crypts?"

"I do. Yes. It was our favorite game. We played it all the time. Primrose loved that game."

"She loved it until the day Jacob answered her knock and scared the Hades out of her. It was the next day she started hanging her ribbons and hearts. Don't you see? She's trying to make our woods into a beautiful place, because it frightens her. She doesn't belong here."

Gothel sighed. "But it's already a beautiful place."

"Primrose doesn't think so," said Hazel with a sad smile.

"Well, I would never make her stay if she really wanted to go, Hazel. Of course, if she wants to leave, we should let her, but not while Mother is still alive. She would never allow it. Do you know what it means for a witch of our blood to leave the dead woods? They can never return. We will have to wipe her memory of this place and of us."

"After Mother is gone, we can do things our own way, Gothel."

"That's true. Maybe. Can we decide how to handle it when the time comes? Together?"

Hazel smiled. "All right, then. We'll decide together."

CHAPTER VI

BLACK CELLOPHANE SKY

Gothel, Primrose, and Hazel were standing outside the conservatory, holding hands and waiting for their mother to come out to tell them it was time for the ceremony. There was a chill in the air that made them shiver and huddle close together. The sky resembled black cellophane with tiny pinholes of light, and the moon was a thin shining crescent. None of it looked quite real. It was like a paper cutout. It was too perfect to have such a remarkable witch's moon on that night. The perfect moon for that sort of magic. And there was something inexplicable in the air. The dead woods felt different to the witches on that night, but they couldn't figure out how.

"The woods feel alive," said Hazel. "Somehow they feel alive."

"The woods *are* alive, my dear Hazel."

Manea came out to greet her daughters. She had artfully arranged her hair in a high elaborate configuration of large curls and golden rapunzel flowers. It had been many years since the sister witches had seen their mother so formally dressed. She wore a golden floor-length empire-waisted gown with long full sleeves that shimmered in the light, and her skin also glowed, like she had bathed in rapunzel flower dust. She didn't look at all like the mother they knew. She looked younger, and somehow more majestic than they had ever seen her.

"You've always felt so much—too much, in fact. It's the singular aspect about you that has always caused me trepidation, but I see now it will work in your favor. Always trust your feelings, Hazel. They are your guides. You feel the vibrations of the world around you. You feel the emotions of others more profoundly than anyone else I've met, even with only a small amount of my blood within you. You even feel the dead."

"The dead?" Primrose looked around nervously, trying to find the dead, but all she could see was endless darkness.

"Yes, my dear child. The dead." Manea took her gaze from her bewildered daughters and looked toward the dense part of the forest, where her creatures were waiting for her. "Come, my love, and bring my children forth so they may behold the future queens of the dead!"

The tall grotesquerie Manea had called her love stepped out of the shadows as if walking through a pitch-black curtain of night. His trousers and long coat hung on his lanky skeletal body like rags, and the leathery skin stretched over his skull glistened in the light from the open conservatory door. He was surrounded by innumerable skeletal creatures, their numbers stretching for miles into the densest parts of the forest. They were silent, morose creatures, standing almost entirely still, waiting for instructions from their leader. The lanky creature raised his hand, motioning to the skeletal minions to make a pathway, parting the sea of skeletons down the center. The witches couldn't see what was making its way toward them, but they could hear something. It was a choir of little whimpers, the chattering of tiny voices, their pitch full of fear and muffled by sobs.

"Come! Come, my little ones. Welcome. Behold your future queens!" To the young witches' horror, they saw what was coming out of the darkness: the children from the village.

The children slowly made their way through the sea of skeletons while huddled around a ghastly woman with putrid skin that was deeply bruised. The poor woman had a vacant, terrified look on her face, her bulbous eyes darting around, taking in the scene. She didn't seem to notice the horrified children huddled around her, or their tiny hands grasping at her, trying to hold on to her.

"What's wrong with the children's eyes?" wondered Primrose, her voice barely a whisper.

The children's eyes were covered in what looked like dried tar. It was black, shiny, and set into the hollows of their eye sockets. The young witches had never seen anything so horrifying. The sight of the poor children, with their fresh wounds and bruised little bodies, broke their hearts.

"Is this woman . . . are these children . . . are they from the village? You . . . killed them?" asked Primrose, trembling and fumbling her words.

"Calm yourself, Daughter. They would be even more terrified if they could see," said Manea off-handedly.

"You're a monster!" sneered Primrose, looking at her mother with utter contempt.

"What would you have me do? All of our creatures must be in attendance. They must be bound to you."

"They are not creatures! They're children! Children you killed! And now you're parading them around for your amusement. It's disgusting! I won't have anything to do with it," yelled Primrose.

"This is our life, Primrose! Stop being weak! You will take the blood, and you will help your sisters uphold our traditions. And you will never leave the dead woods! Do you understand? I do not want to hear another word from you, not one—not until it's time to recite your portion of the ceremony!"

Primrose said nothing. Disgusted and horrified, she just looked at her mother as the dead children cried even harder at the sound of Manea's angry voice.

"Not another word, Primrose! Or I will truly make these children suffer!"

Primrose's anger and revulsion writhed within her, but she choked down her words.

"Direct your anger there, Primrose!" Manea pointed her bony finger at the woman standing with the children and gave her a wrathful look. "If she had agreed to the terms, these children wouldn't be here! She wanted to be with her precious dead so desperately! To surround herself by death! Well, now she shall be! Forever! These children's blood is on her hands! Not mine!"

The dead woman flinched, grasping the hand of a little girl in a tattered bloodstained dress and pulling her closer, as if the blind child could shield her from the queen's wrath.

"Mother, please, stop!" pleaded Hazel.

Manea whipped her head around like a deadly viper to look at Hazel.

"Do you think I like ending the lives of children and bringing them here? It's unnatural to end a life so young. They find it so much harder to transition and to accept that they have passed. I've covered their eyes to make it easier for them, Hazel."

"Mother, they're in pain. They're suffering."

Manea looked to the lanky skeletal creature. "My love, does it hurt to be dead?"

"No, my queen, not anymore."

"See! They will be fine! Now calm down. After the ceremony, the children will be put in their graves and won't be woken until their transition, which is the usual custom, barring special circumstances like our ceremony."

"Will they know they're in their graves? Will they be in pain?"

"No, Hazel, my flower, they won't. However, since this woman would rather see the little ones dead than agree to the terms, she will be granted no peace."

The woman let out a howling guttural moan, causing the children to cry out.

"Silence!" Manea flicked her hand toward the woman, filling her mouth with a thick putrid tar. The woman tried to call out again, but it only made her choke and gasp for breath. "Stop your infernal screaming, woman!"

"Gothel, make her stop!" Primrose pleaded with her sister. Gothel stood frozen, hard as stone, watching the scene, watching her mother to see what she would do.

Hazel took Primrose's hand in hers and gripped it tight. "Primrose, please. Stop talking. If you don't stop these theatrics, Mother is going to do something terrible to those children." Primrose didn't seem to hear her sister; her gaze was still locked on her mother. Hazel took her by the shoulders, shaking her slightly. "Prim! Listen to me! I promise you, promise you, Prim, everything will be okay."

Primrose shook with anger and fear and whispered, "How can you say that? Nothing is ever going to be okay ever again!"

Hazel looked into Primrose's eyes. "Do you trust me?"

"I do."

"Then, please, Primrose, trust me now. I promise you everything will be fine," Hazel said just as a blinding golden light erupted around them.

Hazel wondered if her little sister Primrose was right. She wondered if anything would ever be okay again.

CHAPTER VII

The Primrose Path

The brilliant golden light erupted from the conservatory, illuminating the dead forest. It was more impressive even than the legendary Lighthouse of the Gods. It could be seen well beyond the boundaries of the dead woods, and it struck fear into the hearts of the villagers nearby.

The young witches stood in the center of the room, before their mother. They were surrounded by peering skeletal faces looking in on them from outside the conservatory. The witches had never seen their forest so animated, so alive, and they had never seen their mother looking quite so dignified in all their years with her.

Manea's skin was glowing in the light of the flowers as she reached for her small sickle knife hanging from her belt on a long silver chain. She sliced open her hand, cutting it deeply. The blood dripped down her long bone-thin arm onto her golden dress as her daughters looked at her with fear and wonder.

"My daughters! From this night forth, and upon my passing, those who languish in the woods will be bound to you by my blood!"

Manea pushed her hair back from her face, smearing blood onto her forehead and into her hair. She raised her hands, opening the skylight to reveal the inky black sky with tiny silver pinholes of light. "Girls, give me your hands." The young witches reached out their trembling hands, exposing their palms. "Put your hands together," their mother snapped. The witches quickly did as their mother said, moving their hands together, each slightly overlapping the other—and before they could react, their mother sliced open their palms in one quick unceremonious slash. Primrose screamed and jerked her hand away, clutching it to her chest, smearing blood on her bodice.

Manea put a large silver bowl on the floor to catch Hazel's and Gothel's blood. There it mingled with Manea's. "Primrose, you must mingle your blood with ours."

Primrose cried silently, clutching her hand. "I can't, Mother, I can't!"

Manea grabbed Primrose's hand and squeezed it over the bowl, mingling Primrose's blood with Gothel's, Hazel's, and her own. "Now stand back!" she said, picking up the bowl.

Manea raised the bowl above her head, offering it to the sky. The blood exploded, filling the air with crimson luminescence, and drifted up through the skylight and into the clouds, turning them and the stars a deep bloodred that glistened like tiny fragments of rubies.

Manea set down the bowl and stretched out her long bony fingers, her hands shaking with her power as lightning exploded from her fingertips, causing the clouds to burst and rain blood on the dead woods, the witches, and her skeletal minions.

"With this blood, the dead are now bound to us all. The four of us. Forever!"

Primrose screamed again, falling to the floor, and wept uncontrollably, violently shaking with each sob. "I can't do this! I can't."

Gothel picked up her sister and held her tightly in her arms. "Prim! Calm down, please."

Primrose looked terrified, her face speckled with blood. "I'm sorry, Gothel, I can't do this! I thought I could. I tried. I promise."

"Silence!" Manea roughly took Primrose by the hair with one hand and covered her mouth with her bleeding hand. "You will take my blood!" screamed Manea as Primrose flailed, trying to fight off her mother. Manea was too strong; she forced Primrose to the ground, still pressing her bleeding hand over Primrose's open mouth, muffling her screams as Primrose kicked, trying to get her mother off her. Gothel and Hazel stood, paralyzed with fear, as they watched their sister convulse, trying to wriggle out from under their mother while spitting blood into her face.

Manea stood up and wiped her face, looking down on her daughter, splayed on the floor. "You think I don't know your heart, Primrose? Look at you! Too weak to even take my blood! You're pathetic! Even your sisters see your flaws. Even they considered letting you leave the dead woods, because they know you would only be a hindrance to them! Well, I will save them the heartbreak of seeing you leave!" Manea stretched out her long spindly hands, clutching at the air, squeezing something within them. Primrose started to cough, grasping at her throat. Gothel couldn't believe what she was seeing.

Her mother was killing Primrose.

"Mother, stop!" screamed Hazel. Manea flicked her hand in Hazel's direction, sending her careering across the room and through one of the conservatory windows, the glass shattering and mixing with Hazel's blood. "Hazel!" Gothel didn't know which sister to run to, Hazel or Primrose. She felt helpless and afraid.

Primrose is dying. Her face was turning purple, her eyes large and bulbous. She was on the edge of death, somewhere between there and the mists. Gothel didn't know how to stop her mother. She hadn't taken the blood. She had no powers. And then she remembered. *The flowers. Mother's treasures!* She seized one of the oil lamps that hung on hooks around the room, and screamed at her mother.

"Mother, stop! Stop or I will burn it all down!"

Manea stopped dead. She looked up from Primrose and saw Gothel standing in the center of the flowers, holding the oil lamp. "Gothel, no! You'll kill us all! Put down the lamp!"

"Not until you let Primrose go!"

"Take her!" said Manea, tossing Primrose onto the floor in a bloody heap. "Take your pathetic excuse for a sister! I don't want her!" Manea stepped away from Primrose. "Take her out of here now before I change my mind and kill you all! Get out of here! Now!"

Gothel rushed to her sister and tried to rouse her. "Prim, can you walk? Let's get out of here!"

Primrose got up, wobbly on her feet, and let her

sister guide her out of the conservatory to where Hazel was lying on the ground. Manea stood stark still, waiting and watching from the conservatory window to see what Gothel would do.

"Hazel, are you okay?" Gothel helped the bloodied and bruised Hazel to her feet, all the while keeping an eye on her mother. "Don't you move, Mother! Or I will do it!" Gothel said in her most commanding voice.

The three sisters stood there for what felt like an eternity, just looking at their mother. Gothel had to wonder how the three of them looked, standing there. Did they look afraid? Did her mother think she was brave? Whatever her mother thought was not betrayed by the stone expression on her face. *I think she is more afraid than we are.*

"You have to kill her," Hazel said under her breath.

"You have to!" said Primrose, still clutching her bruised throat.

"Silence, you wretched vipers!" said Manea, sending Hazel and Primrose flying with her magic and smashing them against a tree, splintering it into bits.

"Mother, stop! Please don't kill us!"

Manea's face utterly changed. She looked like an animal trying to make out a strange noise. "Kill you, Gothel? Never! I could never hurt you! Haven't you been listening to me? Haven't you read it in my journals? To hurt you would be like hurting myself! I could never hurt you, even if I wanted to!"

"Then please leave my sisters alone. Please! Don't hurt them anymore!"

"Sisters?" Manea laughed. "Ha! They're nothing to you, Gothel! Hazel had promise. I wanted her to be your companion in magic. I wanted her to be your guide, to help you feel, because your heart is too much like mine. Too black. Hazel would be able to help you in matters of the heart. And Primrose, well, I thought she would be a welcome distraction from your studies, something to break the monotony and toiling, but that's all they are to you, Gothel! You, Gothel, you are mine!"

"Then please don't break my heart. Please don't kill them!" screamed Gothel.

"It's too late. Primrose will never agree to stay in the dead woods, and Hazel will talk you into letting her leave, putting our home in danger. Putting everything at risk! I can't let that happen. I can't let them destroy everything my family has created and cultivated here. Everything that will someday belong to you! I'm sorry, my darling, but they have to die."

"No, Mother! *You have to die!*" Gothel hurled the lamp into the conservatory, setting the rapunzel aflame.

"Gothel! What have you done?" Manea created a protective shield around herself so the flames couldn't touch her. "Gothel! No! Save the rapunzel!" Manea screamed as she started to wither and age and crumble to dust. She screamed in pain as the rapunzel burned. "Gothel! Save the rapunzel!"

The flames overtook the conservatory. Gothel snatched up one of the rapunzel flowers before the conservatory started to collapse, as her mother turned to dust, crumbling before her eyes. Gothel watched in horror as her mother withered into a dry husk and disintegrated.

"Gothel! Please help me!" screamed her mother right before her face fell to dust.

I killed her. I killed her! Gothel's head was spinning. She couldn't believe she had done this. She wanted to take it back. She wanted to try to reason with her. Give her a chance. But it was too late. Everything was destroyed. Everything was in ruins.

Sisters!

Gothel ran from the burning conservatory into the dead woods. She ran past the blood-soaked legion of the dead into the trees, searching for her sisters, calling out their names, panicked her mother had killed them. "Primrose! Hazel? Where are you?" She begged the morose skeletal creatures to help her find them and was answered with vacant looks. "Have you seen my sisters?" The skeletons just stared, showing no sign they even noticed their mistress had died. *Where is Jacob?* she thought. "Jacob! Primrose! Hazel!" She screamed again and again as she ran into the darkness with only the light of the flower and the burning conservatory in the distance to guide her.

Chapter VIII

Gothel's Plan

Gothel stood alone on the balcony off the library overlooking the destroyed conservatory. It was still smoldering, sending tiny wisps of smoke into the air. It was a cold morning, and the tops of the dead trees were obscured in a heavy mist and choked with gray smoke and ash. The forest was silent and still, as the dead woods always were, but that day it seemed even more unnatural than usual. Gothel couldn't shake the horrible vision of her mother dying. No matter how hard she tried to banish the vile images, she couldn't help seeing her mother cry out in pain as her face became dust. It was the worst thing she had ever witnessed. *I did that to her. I killed my own mother.*

She couldn't imagine what that must have felt like, and it sent a horrible feeling throughout her entire body. She felt sick and trapped within herself, as if she would never escape the feeling of dread and guilt. She wanted to go to the burnt structure and find her mother's remains—she wanted to put them somewhere safe—but she couldn't bring herself to do it. She was afraid. She had no idea what to do now. She and Hazel hadn't taken her mother's blood. Only Primrose was given it. By force. Gothel wasn't given her mother's magic. She was defenseless. They were alone. And it was up to Gothel to make sure they were taken care of.

"Gothel! Did you sleep at all?" It was Hazel. She was standing on the threshold of the balcony. "Come inside. It's cold out there."

"I can't."

"What do you mean you can't? Come inside." Hazel walked out to meet her sister and saw that Gothel was looking at the ruins of the conservatory. "She's not going to rise from the ashes, Gothel. All of the rapunzel was destroyed."

"Not all of it," said Gothel, taking one small flower from the pocket of her dress.

"That's not enough to bring her back, is it?" asked Hazel, fearful her mother's spirit could somehow use the flower to rise from the dead.

"I'm not worried about Mother coming back. I'm worried about us. I'm worried about how we're going to survive without her. Without her blood. Without her powers." Gothel stood there a moment, looking at the smoldering ashes below. "I thought I'd lost you forever last night, Hazel. You and Primrose. It was terrifying finding you lying there in the darkness so still and so quiet. I thought you were dead."

"But we're fine, Gothel. And we're home. We're together. Together forever."

Sisters. Together forever.

Gothel smiled. And then she remembered. "Wait! Primrose! She has Mother's blood. Some of it, at least. We can do the ceremony again when she's recovered. Then we won't be so defenseless!"

"Gothel! We can't put her through that! Not

after what Mother did to her! Not after everything we went through last night."

"We have no choice, Hazel! We have to! You didn't see what happened to Mother! The way she died was horrible, and the same thing will happen to us if we don't replant this flower and learn Mother's magic."

"Or we can destroy it and the entire forest and leave this place forever! Live normal lives without magic. There is nothing for us here, Gothel! Nothing! There is no magic to learn now that Mother is gone."

"Primrose has some of Mother's magic! She forced her to drink the blood! Maybe it's enough, Hazel! Promise me we won't give up. Please. Let's just talk to Primrose about it when she's feeling better. I promise we'll only do it if she agrees. I promise I won't force her."

"But we still don't know how to do the ceremony even if she agrees!"

"We still have all of Mother's books. All her spells. Her history. The history of our ancestors! Everything is not lost! I can replant the flower and we can start again. We can still have the life we imagined. Please?"

"Okay, Gothel. As long as Prim doesn't mind doing the ceremony."

"What ceremony?" It was Primrose. She was standing in the center of the library in the shadow of a large stone bat hanging from the rafters. She looked drawn and pale in her white nightdress, and the cuts and bruises on her face and neck were all the more striking in contrast to her pallor.

"Prim! What are you doing out of bed?" scolded Hazel, running to her sister.

"I'm fine, Hazel. I promise! What were you two talking about?"

Hazel and Gothel just looked at Primrose. They weren't ready to have that conversation right then— and they knew Primrose wasn't ready to hear what they had to say.

"What? What is it?" Primrose insisted.

"Nothing, Prim. We can talk about it later. Let's go downstairs and have some breakfast," said Hazel, patting her hand.

"No, I want you to tell me what you were talking about right now!" Primrose put her hands on her hips and gave her sisters her infamous *I'm very serious* look.

"Gothel and I were discussing our options."

"What options are those?" Primrose was clearly starting to get annoyed.

"Staying here in the dead woods or going into the world," said Hazel, looking at Gothel.

"Well, we should go, of course! I don't want to stay here!" said Primrose. "Why in Hades would we stay?"

Gothel sighed.

"What? You want to stay?" Primrose scoffed and continued. "*Of course* you want to stay! Well, you can stay if you want! You can stay forever for all I care, but I'm leaving! And I think Hazel wants to come with me!"

"Hazel wants to stay with me, Prim! And I wish you would, too! I need you both," said Gothel as sweetly as she could, trying hard not to upset her sister even more than she already was.

"Gothel was hoping you'd be willing to share Mother's blood with us, Prim. That way we would all have her powers. At least some of them, anyway."

"Oh really? That's why you need me? For Mother's blood! What's happened to you, Gothel? What in Hades is wrong with you? Fine! I'll share Mother's blood with you, but I'm not staying here. I will not stay in a place that houses dead children! I will not stay here and watch you turn into Mother! I don't want any part of this sick fantasy you have in your head, the three of us being witches together. Doing magic. And controlling those things out there! Those children! Those dead children! You don't think I saw you last night commanding them to their graves after you found me and Hazel? You don't think I saw the look on your face when they followed your orders? You looked like Mother! Just like her, Gothel! And I won't stay here watching you become more like her every day!"

"Then why are you sharing her blood with me, Prim? Why not just leave now?"

"Because! I need you to find the spell that lets

me out of this place, and I know you won't go with me no matter how much I beg! And as much as I want to hate you, I can't! I love you, and I won't just leave you here defenseless! With nothing. Now go to Mother's books and figure out how we do the ceremony."

"Now?" asked Gothel in shock. *This isn't how it was supposed to go.* She wasn't ready to lose Primrose. She wasn't ready to say good-bye. Not like this. Not with Primrose hating her.

"Yes, now! We will do it tonight," spat Primrose.

"That's not enough time, Prim!" said Gothel.

"Well, it had better be, because I'm leaving at midnight either way, even if I have to use Mother's powers to blast my way through the thicket!" Primrose turned to leave the room.

"Prim, no! It's not enough time. Please!" Gothel begged.

Primrose laughed. "You're more like Mother than you even realize, Gothel. You don't care if I'm leaving. You only care that you won't have enough time to work out how to do the blood ceremony before I go!" She left the room, slamming the door behind her and leaving Gothel gobsmacked.

"That's not true! You know it's not true. It's not like she can leave anyway, not if I can't find the spell."

Hazel had tears sliding down her face. "I'm not so sure, Gothel. I'm going after Prim. Good luck finding Mother's spell."

Gothel stood alone in the library. She felt a terrible chill and wondered if her sisters were right.

Was she really like her mother?

No! They were sisters. *Together forever.* Wasn't that the promise? It was Primrose who was breaking their vow. It was Primrose who was ruining everything!

Gothel grabbed her cloak, which was lying on the back of her favorite leather chair, threw it on, and left the library. The stone mansion was chilly that morning. She could feel the coolness of the stone floors penetrating her house slippers. The cold there was the coldness of death, and she hated it. *We need to buy some rugs, some tapestries,* Gothel thought.

She had never understood why her mother hadn't thought to make a proper home for them, why she was content to live in such a barren, cold place, always in the shadows of night creatures peering at them from the darkness.

Maybe if I made this a real home, Primrose would want to stay, she thought. *I could let Primrose buy whatever she wants. We could make this place a real home, a beautiful place that she couldn't possibly leave. And maybe she would be happy again.*

Maybe.

Gothel went upstairs to her mother's room. It was dark, all the curtains were drawn, and it was damp from the cold and mist outside. She felt strange going into her mother's room. The air was thick and stale, and there was a faint smell of her mother. It made her queasy. Gothel realized she had never really spent time there, in her mother's room. The deep crimson sheer curtains hanging from the four-poster made the room even darker. She could almost see her mother sleeping there in her bed. *No, it's a trick of the light.* She took a deep breath and looked around the room, trying to banish the image of her mother from her mind. The room was bare, like the rest of the house. It was drafty, without mirrors or furnishings of any kind aside from the four-poster, a desk at the window, and a little round table at her bedside. It seemed sad now, the empty room. Gothel almost forgot why she had gone up there.

The key.

It's probably in the desk. Gothel went to her mother's desk and opened the tiny drawer in the center. There it was: the key to Mother's vault. She slipped it into the pocket of her cloak and left the room quickly. She couldn't stand to be there much longer. She felt as if someone was watching her. As if her mother was there, telling her to get out.

As she left the room, she turned back to look at the bed again. And for a moment she thought she saw her mother standing there at the foot of the bed, her eyes blazing with anger.

"What are you doing?" It was Hazel. She was standing in the doorway.

"What? Oh! Hazel."

"What's wrong, Gothel? Did you see something?"

"I thought I did. Never mind. How's Prim?"

"She's fine. But she's serious, Gothel. She wants to leave."

"I know. But I have a plan!" Gothel smiled.

Hazel smiled, too. "You do, don't you? Do you think it will work?"

"I hope it does! I really want Primrose to stay— and not just because I want to take over for Mother. I want you both to stay because we vowed to be together forever. I love you."

"Then you'd better tell me about this plan. What can I do to help?"

Chapter IX

The Key

Gothel, Hazel, and Primrose stood at the boundary of the dead woods. They rarely came that close to the thicket. They could see the villages in the distance and couldn't help wondering what the people in those villages thought of the dreaded witches of the dead woods.

"Are you sure about this, Gothel?" asked Primrose.

"I am. Look." Gothel had one of her mother's books in her hand. It was open to the page that showed the spell to open a portal through the rose-bush thicket. "We saw her do it, Prim. She squeezed her hand just like it's illustrated here in the book. Look! Like this!"

"I see it, Gothel! But what am I supposed to do?"

"Concentrate! Think about what you're trying to accomplish. Envision the red glowing ball that will open the thicket."

"I don't know, Gothel."

"Prim, please! Do you want to get out of here? Do you want to see the world? We talked about this! I want you to make this place beautiful, make it a place you would want to stay in forever. We've lived in this dreary mansion our entire lives. It's like a dead place. It's not a home. Mother never made it beautiful, she was always so focused on her magic. I want you to bring it to life, Prim! I want you to decorate it with color. I want you to love it."

Primrose laughed. "What happened to you?"

"What do you mean?"

Hazel smiled at both of her sisters. "Gothel wants us to stay because she loves us, Prim. She wants to keep our vow. Sisters together forever. And she wants to make a beautiful home for us. And the only way to do that is to get through that thicket."

"It's true, Prim! I really do!"

"I know you do. I can tell. It's just . . ."

"What?"

"You seem like your old self again. Like the Gothel I love. That's all." Primrose took a breath. "Okay, let's try to do this spell." She looked again at the book Gothel was holding. "So, is this right?" She was holding her hand the way it was illustrated in their mother's spell book.

"Yes. That's right. Now just think about creating a red ball that you can use to open the thicket."

"Okay," said Primrose, not convinced it would work. She reached out her hand and closed it on something invisible. "Oh! I can feel something! I can feel something small, but I can't see it! Can you see it?"

"That's amazing, Prim! You can feel the ball in your hand?" asked Gothel, feeling giddy.

"I can!" said Primrose, laughing, excited that the spell was working.

"Visualize the ball, Prim! Make it solid!" Gothel said.

A tiny ball of light appeared in Primrose's hand. It was wispy and silver, almost like smoke.

"Ah! Look! I made something! Should I throw it? Should I throw it?" asked Primrose, afraid to hold it in her hand too long.

"No! Imagine it larger, make it red," urged Gothel.

Primrose screwed up her face. Her cheeks were flushed and splotchy from straining so hard. "I can't! It won't turn red."

"Concentrate, Prim!" said Gothel. "Concentrate!"

"Ow!" Prim flicked her hand the way her mother had the night she opened the thicket. It sent the wispy silver ball into the rosebush thicket, where it dispersed the moment it made impact.

"Prim!"

"I'm sorry! I tried. I really did, but it started to burn my hand."

"That's okay, we can try again," said Gothel, determined to make the spell work.

"Let's try later, Gothel. Prim is tired."

Gothel sighed. "I'm happy you tried, Prim.

Don't worry, we'll figure out how to get out of here. I promise. Let's have some breakfast." The sisters walked the long path of dead weeping willows, passing the ruined conservatory as they made their way to their mansion on the hill. "I was thinking. Maybe we should do something with Mother's ashes."

Primrose shot Gothel a disapproving look, but Hazel answered. "I think Gothel is right. We should do something with Mother's ashes. We should put her to rest. I think we should build something in the conservatory's place, something beautiful so our minds don't always go to that horrible night every time we pass it."

"I guess you're right," said Primrose. "That's a good idea, Hazel."

"Well, who wants breakfast?" asked Hazel, leading her sisters back to their house. "We have scones waiting for us."

The house seemed heavy with their mother's memory. More than ever Gothel thought she had made the right decision to let Primrose decorate the house as she wished. Not only would she have her sisters; she would have the time she needed to work out the blood ritual, since Primrose had agreed to stay. Now they just needed to figure out how to get the thicket open so they could get the things they would need to make their somber mansion a home—a home she and her sisters would share forever.

The sister witches sat at the long wooden table in the dining room. It was a deep cherry wood. The only decorations in the barren room were carvings of ravens on the walls and over the archways. There was a blazing fire in the large stone fireplace, which had a mantel supported by two enormous statues crafted to look like dead trees with ravens perched in their branches. It was a cavernous room with many windows, open to the elements, overlooking the dead woods and the graves of their mother's minions. The entire landscape was bleak, with its gray sky, black trees, and white headstones.

The sisters just sat there, silently staring at the plate of scones on the table, which was littered with dried leaves that had blown in from the windows. The scones were untouched, with the hazelnut butter and preserves sitting beside them.

"We have to figure out how to open the thicket. Our pantries are full now, but we will have to refill them at some point," said Hazel.

"I don't even know where Mother went to get all our supplies. I mean, I don't recall her ever leaving the dead woods, do you?"

"I wonder. Do you think the tall creature Jacob would know?" asked Gothel.

"I don't know, Gothel. I'd rather never wake them again," said Primrose, finally taking one of the scones and putting it on a small gray plate edged with silver.

"I understand," said Gothel, not wanting to upset her sister by saying she didn't agree with her. She quickly changed the subject, directing their conversation to the house renovations. "We should have shutters made for these windows, don't you think?

I never understood why mother wanted this room open to the outside. What do you think, Prim? Shutters?"

"I think that's a good idea. We can open them when we want to let in the light."

"Yes! You know, I'm going to find Mother's journals and see if there is something written about the thicket, and where she got our food and other supplies. Hazel, can you take an inventory and see how long our current supplies will last?"

"Good idea, Gothel," said Hazel.

"And, Prim, would you like to go around the house and make notes on everything we will need to make the house as you would like it? Furniture, drapes, paintings, statues—you name it—whatever your heart desires."

"Do we really have enough gold to do all of that?" asked Primrose.

"Gothel has the key," said Hazel.

"The key?" asked Primrose.

"Yes, she has the key to Mother's fortune."

"I suppose it's our fortune now." Gothel smiled.

She never paused to wonder where the money came from, and it seemed never to run out. "Don't worry, Sisters. We will make a beautiful life here. I promise we will make this place our home."

CHAPTER X

SIR JACOB
OF THE DEAD

Gothel walked the long winding path that led from the conservatory to the dense part of the dead woods she and her sisters called the city of the dead. It was nice to stretch her legs after many hours of reading her mother's books, trying to find another way to get past the thicket, and something told her Jacob had the answers she needed. She walked past endless tombstones and crypts lining the little pathways and creating a sort of labyrinth. There was no breeze that day, so the weeping willows' branches were still, obscuring the gray sky and letting in very little light. The path was littered with dried leaves and broken branches that crunched under Gothel's feet as she made her way to the creature's crypt. It was as if she had always known where he rested, her feet guiding her right to his doorstep. His crypt was more beautiful than the others in the city; it was larger, more like a little house with its stained glass windows and weeping angel to the right of the stone door. She wondered if he had made a home for himself in there. She wondered how he spent his time. She imagined him sitting at a little round wooden table, with a single candle, writing a love letter to her mother.

Gods, what am I doing here?

She knew her sisters would be upset if they found out she had come to see the creature, but something within her told her he would have the answers to her questions. And since he was now bound to Gothel and her sisters, he would have to answer her truthfully. Or at least that was what it said in her mother's book. There was an interesting passage in one of her mother's journals that called him by name: Sir Jacob. *To know his name is to have power over him. To know his name means he can do you no harm.* According to her mother's books, he wasn't like the other creatures that were bound to the witches of the woods. Something about him was different, and Gothel intended to find out what that was.

Her mother had called the creature her love, and it occurred to Gothel that her mother might have actually loved the man.

She had so many questions she wanted to ask her mother. There was so much she didn't know. After years of neglect, leaving Gothel and her sisters to wander the woods alone, motherless while she was doing her magic, she was now gone without passing her magic on to her daughters, with no legacy of witches to take her place. Gothel suddenly felt the burden of guilt, not only for killing her mother but for sending her family and their legacy into ruins.

Gothel stood before Jacob's crypt, its stained glass window adorned with a large red anatomically designed heart. The angel sat before the creature's stone doorway, splayed on the marble slab, weeping into the crook of her arm, her wings flat against her naked body, giving the poor angel her dignity. Gothel had never noticed before, but the angel looked a bit like her mother, with her long hair and slender frame. It was eerie seeing an image that looked so much like her mother weeping. She had never seen her mother cry, not in all their years, until the previous night. The night of her death. There was so much about her mother she didn't know, even beyond practical matters like where she got their food or how she did her magic. Gothel knew nothing about her at all, unless she had read it in one of her books. Maybe her mother had slipped away in the night when Gothel and her sisters slept. She could have had an entire life Gothel didn't know about. She certainly hadn't spent it with her daughters, except to swoop in on them occasionally with little gifts to appease them and keep them occupied. But where had she gotten those things? Prim's scissors and Hazel's paper? She clearly had gone out of the dead woods often for all those little things. Could she really have been so consumed by magic there was nothing else in her life? Nothing but necromancy, cultivating the flowers, death, and resurrection?

Gothel sighed. And she knocked on the creature's crypt door. *Maybe Jacob will know.*

"Sir Jacob, rise. Your queen is in need of you."

The crypt door opened slowly. The sound of stone rubbing against stone was unnerving to her; it set her teeth on edge and filled her body with a strange tingling sensation that made her feel trapped within herself.

He stepped out of the crypt, his feet shuffling among the dried leaves and twigs. Sir Jacob was even taller than the image Gothel had of him in her mind. And his skull seemed remarkably larger than the average male's head. He was enormous, this man; the size of his hands alone was twice that of hers, if not more. She wondered what this man had looked like when he was alive. He must have had a long narrow face with high pronounced cheekbones, and his eyes, still intact, looked as if they might have been blue, though now they were cloudy and white.

"Yes, my queen's daughter. How may I serve you?" said Jacob in a voice that sounded remarkably human. Remarkably soothing.

"Sir Jacob. I have some questions I hope you can answer. My mother died before she could instruct us. We have no idea—"

"I understand. You don't need to go on. Your mother anticipated you would come to me should anything ever happen to her. The first order of business is to put her at rest. She is trapped within the woods, waiting to be released into the mists that are waiting for her. Your ancestors are there, waiting for you to do the ceremony to send her spirit to be among them."

"They're here? Waiting?"

"Yes."

"Are they angry with me for killing Mother?"

"That is not for me to say, little witch. But they have agreed to exchange your mother's spirit for the knowledge you need to survive and thrive within the dead woods. Continuing the legacy is their priority, not revenge. Your mother spent a lot of time in this world, her life was not cut short. But you do need her knowledge and you need her blood if you're going to rule here in her place."

"But she was destroyed in the fire, all of her blood is gone."

"Not all of it, little witch. That key you have in your pocket opens the vault. Within it you'll find more than her fortune. There is a chest that contains your mother's blood, and her spell book with the instructions you will need to take her blood. The chest is behind a secret door that can be opened by pressing the seventh stone from the top. But the blood is only for you, Gothel. Don't share it with your sisters. That is your mother's command."

"It doesn't matter what my mother commands!"

The specter nodded slightly. "I am bound to you and have to serve you no matter. I can only offer my advice, you are not required to take it."

"What were you to my mother?"

"That is between me and your mother, little witch," said the creature with something that resembled a twisted sad smile.

"I'm sorry, Jacob. I shouldn't have asked you that."

"Not to worry, little witch. Do you have more questions for me?" said Jacob with the same sneer-like smile. Gothel was starting to understand that was simply what happened when he smiled. His skin was so tightly stretched across his face that it distorted when he smiled or spoke. She found it oddly charming and wondered again what the man had looked like when he was alive.

"Do you know how Mother left the dead woods? To get things we needed for the house, like food, supplies?" she finally asked after realizing she had been staring at him for longer than would be considered polite.

"Those things are delivered by a neighboring village. A family that has worked in the world for us for many generations. They bring the supplies every new moon. If there is something you want, you only need to tell me, and I will be sure they fetch it."

"So she never left the dead woods?"

"Never. Not that I am aware of, at any rate."

"And you? How do you leave?"

"Your mother created an invisible portal for me to come and go as I please. But it only allows me access. No one else may pass through it. What is it that you need?"

"I wanted to take my sisters into the world. To buy furnishings for the house. I want to make it beautiful so they will stay."

"I will take care of that for you, Gothel. I will take care of it all. Please don't ever try to leave the dead woods. You're not meant to go beyond the thicket. That is why I am here. Your place is here."

Sir Jacob's eyes rolled back into his head, and he convulsed and started to sputter. *"The station riders are far behind, the secret voices I cannot find. The stench of Hades is taunting me, and still those voices I cannot see."*

"What? What are you saying? What's wrong, Sir Jacob?"

"Gothel! You betrayed me! If it wouldn't anger our ancestors, I would make this forest rise to destroy you and your precious sisters! But I will not lose my place among my family and be forever doomed to haunt these lands. The

satisfaction of seeing you and your sisters dead isn't worth my eternal damnation."

"Mother?"

"Yes, my blackhearted child."

"You gave me no choice! You were going to kill my sisters!"

"There will be time enough to settle this when you've turned to dust and joined me and your ancestors in the mists, but that time is not now. Now we must prepare you to take my place here as queen. The first thing you need to do is replant that rapunzel flower before it dies. Then you need to release me into the mists."

"How am I going to explain all of this to Hazel and Prim? They didn't even want me to call on Sir Jacob. And they're going to be really upset when they find out I've spoken to you."

"Gothel! You are queen of this land! What your sisters think doesn't matter!"

"It matters to me! I want them to stay with me. I want to make them happy."

"So I heard. Very smart of you to make the house beautiful for Prim so she and Hazel will stay with you. I love

that you are still naive enough to think you're doing this for the love of your sisters. Keep thinking that, Gothel, and they will also believe the lies you tell yourself. And forget your plan to do the ceremony with Primrose, she doesn't have enough of my blood to make a difference. Take my blood from the vault and use it only on yourself. If you want your sisters to stay here with you, then you will need to hide your true self from them, as you have been these many days. And you won't be able to do that if you share the blood with them."

"But I want them with me forever!"

"And they will be, with the power of the flower, Gothel. That is what keeps us alive for so long."

"But the necromancy isn't powered by the flower. . . ."

"You're very smart, Gothel. You have my mind. You will learn everything you need to know from my blood, my books, and the knowledge of your ancestors. Listen to me. I may be dead, but Mother still knows best."

"Yes, Mother."

"Good. Go now and plant the flower. And let Jacob handle the mundane tasks. After you've planted the

flower, I will show you how to return me to our ancestors."

Gothel took the flower out of her cloak pocket and looked at it. *Thank the gods it hasn't wilted.*

"No, it lasts longer than other cut flowers, but you can't put off planting it for too much longer. Go on. Jacob will be fine. We will both be waiting for you here when you return."

Gothel turned to leave, but her mother stopped her. *"Oh, and, Gothel, it wasn't a trick of the light."*

"What?"

"Seeing me in my bedroom, seeing my image in the statue. If you don't release me to my ancestors before they go, I will haunt you until the end of your days. I will make this place a living Hades. For you and your sisters."

"Don't worry, Mother. I will send you to the mists."

"Good girl."

Gothel took her time getting back. She needed to think about what she was going to say to her sisters. The dead woods were so still and so close that day, the light so muted by the thick mists, Gothel felt trapped She was overwhelmed by everything she had to do. Replant the flower, send her mother to the mists, explain everything to her sisters, learn Mother's magic . . .

One task at a time. Replant the flower.

When Gothel finally made her way from the city of the dead, she found scores of skeletal creatures tearing down the old conservatory and removing the debris from the area in wooden carts. How was she going to explain that to Hazel and Primrose? She barely knew how to explain it to herself.

One of the creatures was looking directly at her, as if trying to get her attention.

"Yes? May I help you?" she asked the monstrosity.

The creature just stared at her, as if he was looking right through her. She felt stupid talking to him; as far as she knew, the creatures couldn't speak. The creature, who was entirely skeletal, handed Gothel a note and went back to his duties without any ceremony. Gothel found herself thanking the creature, even though she wasn't sure why. The letter was written on white parchment and was sealed with red wax. The stamp in the wax had some sort of knightly crest. She opened the letter and found that it was from Sir Jacob.

Lady Gothel,

I have instructed your creatures to start work on the renovation of the conservatory directly. Please give them any instructions you see fit. They will understand and obey your instructions. Materials needed for the new structure can be ordered by me and will be delivered as soon as it is possible.

I have also sent word to our man in the world to bring all manner of furnishings, tapestries, bedding, statuary, paintings, clothing, and other items I think your sisters would enjoy. Any that are not to your taste can be sent back, and payment will not be required until you have made your final selections. The first of many wagons will start appearing at the mansion in three days' time.

After you have seen to the replanting of the

rapunzel (which can be managed by Victor, the creature who delivered you this missive) and you have successfully given your sisters errands to occupy their time, please make your way back to my crypt, where your mother and I will be waiting.

Eternally yours,
Sir Jacob

Gothel sighed. "Primrose and Hazel are going to freak out when they see this!"

"Primrose might. How about telling me what's going on?"

Gothel turned around to find Hazel standing at the edge of the burnt conservatory.

"Hazel, hi! Where's Primrose?"

"She's running around like a little maniac, deciding how she'd like to decorate the mansion. I'm assuming that's why you gave us our various tasks, to keep us busy while you were ordering Mother's minions about? You know Prim is going to be furious you've awoken them."

"But I didn't! Sir Jacob did!"

"How is that possible, Gothel? Did you wake him?"

"Well . . ."

"Gothel!"

"I didn't have a choice! It turns out he handles everything around here, Hazel, everything!"

"That makes sense. But I think you'd better tell me everything so I know what to say to Prim."

And so she did.

CHAPTER XI

MOTHER'S REVENGE

After searching the entire house, Hazel found Primrose in their mother's room. She was lying on her back, looking up at the ceiling.

"Prim! What are you doing?" asked Hazel.

Primrose sat up. "It's so sad in here, isn't it?"

"Why don't we go down to the library? I hate it in here."

"Don't daughters usually go into their mother's room after she dies, look through her things, and reminisce and think about how much they miss her?"

"In storybooks, sure. Prim, no matter how many

hearts you put in here, it's never going to give us good memories about Mother, or give us the mother we deserved. Come on. I need to talk to you. Let's go down to the library, or the kitchen."

"No, let's talk here. What's going on?"

"Please don't freak out, it's about Gothel."

"Where is she?" asked Primrose.

"She's with Sir Jacob."

"Okay, who's that?"

"Before you say anything at all, can you just promise to listen to me, Prim?"

"Okay . . ."

"Sir Jacob is Mother's creature. Her 'love.'"

"Wait. Didn't we decide she wouldn't talk to him?"

"Well, it was you who decided."

Primrose rolled her eyes.

"Listen to me, Primrose. If we're all going to stay here, there are going to have to be some compromises. And this is one of them. Gothel read in Mother's book there is no way for us out of the thicket."

"What?"

"Calm down and listen to me! The only person who can leave here is Sir Jacob. He does everything around here, and Gothel knew you were going to be disappointed, but she arranged for Jacob to bring wagonloads of things for you to choose from to decorate this house. To make you happy, Prim! She's trying to make you happy and do what's best for this family. You're not always going to like the way she has to do it, but I need you to trust her, Prim. And if you can't trust her, then trust me."

"I always have."

"Come on, can we leave this room? I'm hungry, let's go down to the kitchen."

"Fine! But you're cooking. You know what I'm excited about, Hazel?"

"What's that, little sister?"

But before Primrose could answer, their mother's room was engulfed by a blinding light.

"What the Hades was that?" asked Primrose, unsteady on her feet.

"I don't know," said Hazel, using the doorway to

steady herself. She ran to the window. "Prim, come here. Look at this."

"What is that?"

The sky was filled with a huge swirling black vortex that was consuming the dead trees and heading their direction.

"My gods! Do you think Mother is back?"

"I don't know!"

"Do you feel her, Hazel? Is it her? Come on!"

"I don't know! I don't know! I've been feeling her ever since she died. She imbues this house, the forest, but I didn't want to say anything about it!"

"Hazel, look!"

The vortex was getting closer, devouring everything in its path. The trees, the tombstones, and the remains of the conservatory.

"We have to find Gothel! Come on."

Hazel took Primrose by the hand and they ran down the stairs, speeding past the open windows. They could see the vortex getting closer and closer. When they reached the vestibule, they found a legion of skeletons barring them from leaving the house.

"Oh my gods, Hazel! What's going on?"

Forging a path of destruction, the vortex headed toward the house, consuming the sea of skeletons surrounding it.

"Prim, we have to run! It's coming right for us!"

The girls ran as fast as they could. They didn't dare look back, but they could hear the sounds of the house being torn apart and sucked into the vortex as they ran. "Primrose! Don't look back, just run!"

And then they heard a deafening scream unlike anything they had ever heard before. It was their sister. Gothel stood in the rubble, staring at the eye of the vortex as if daring it to come closer.

"Mother, stop!" she bellowed, putting her hand in front of her like a shield.

A terrible screeching voice echoed in the witches' ears, reverberating throughout the house, crumbling the remains of the stone mansion.

"Stay away from my sisters, you witch!" Gothel

yelled with a resonance in her voice her sisters had never heard before.

"You thought I would let you get away with murdering me and taking my place with these abominations at your side? Then you're a bigger fool than I imagined. You are destined to be alone, Gothel!"

The vortex became smaller, focusing its energy and eye on Primrose and Hazel, bringing them to their knees and making them scream in pain. "Mother, no, don't take them from me, I beg you!"

Manea's laugh filled Hazel's and Primrose's ears, making them bleed. They screamed while Gothel watched in horror.

"Mother, stop!" Gothel screamed, but she knew no matter how much she begged, her mother wouldn't care. She needed to do something to save her sisters. And then she remembered something she had read in one of her mother's spell books, *The Art of Spoken Spell-Craft*. She quickly said the first words that came to mind and wished with all her soul that they would work. *"I call upon the old gods* and the new. Send our mother to the mists. Make our lives anew!"

Manea screamed. "Gothel, stop! No! You don't know what you're doing!" But Gothel kept reciting the words. It was as if they came to her on the winds. As if they came from another world. *"I call upon the old gods and the new. Send our mother to the mists. Make our lives anew!"*

"Gothel, no!" screamed the queen of the dead as the vortex condensed, collapsing, and then exploded, shattering into a thick rancid dust that covered everything in sight.

"Primrose! Hazel! Are you okay?"

Gothel ran to her sisters. They looked like onyx statues, covered in the black dust. *Please don't die! Please don't die.*

"Prim! Hazel?" Gothel was wiping the soot from her sisters' faces. "Prim! Please wake up!" said Gothel, slapping her sister's cheek. "Prim! I said wake up!"

"Gods, Gothel! What's all over you?"

Gothel laughed. *She's alive.* Coughing, Hazel

woke to the sound of Gothel's laugh. "Hazel? Are you okay?"

"I think so. Is Mother gone?"

"I think so," said Gothel, looking around the room, which was entirely covered in thick black dust.

The three sisters sat there, looking at their house. There was a giant hole where their vestibule and staircase used to be. Bones were scattered everywhere, and there were tree branches in the chandeliers.

"Gothel! How did you do that?" asked Hazel, looking at her sister in amazement.

"I honestly don't know."

Gothel looked at her sisters. She had no idea how she had destroyed her mother. She was just happy her sisters hadn't died in the process.

"What are we going to do?" asked Primrose. "Our house is destroyed."

"We will have it rebuilt exactly the way we want!" said Gothel. "We will have a new house and a new life. A beautiful life. I promise you."

"How are we going to do that?" asked Primrose.

"We have Jacob, and Mother's creatures."

"I think they're your creatures now, Gothel," said Hazel.

"I think you're right."

CHAPTER XII

THE MORNING ROOM

The young witches were tucked away in the carriage house while their home was being renovated. Every day brought a new wave of wagons, dozens of them bursting with building materials. Gothel sat at the large window, watching the skeletons unload the wagons as her sisters slept. It had been several months since she had sent her mother to the mists, but her sisters still seemed traumatized and exhausted, spending much of their time in bed or sitting in the courtyard, staring blankly at the minions doing their work. She didn't know how to make them better. How to put their minds at ease. Every day came the same questions: Was Mother really gone? Would she come back? How had Gothel stopped her from killing them?

Gothel didn't know the answers. She was just thankful she hadn't lost them. But as the weeks and months went by, she felt as if she was losing her sisters to their fear and melancholy.

There was a knock at the carriage house door. She quickly answered it, hoping the noise wouldn't wake her sisters. It was Jacob.

"Hello, Sir Jacob."

"Hello, little witch. More wagons have arrived."

"I see that. Thank you for seeing to everything."

"It's my pleasure, little witch." He lingered in the doorway a moment longer.

"Is there anything else you wanted to tell me?" asked Gothel, wondering what Jacob might be up to. It wasn't like him to be idle.

"Yes, a wagon arrived I think you would like to see. Will you please come with me?" said Jacob. He seemed very pleased with himself.

She followed him into the courtyard, marveling at all the beautiful statues and the fountain. "I love the courtyard, Jacob, it's beautiful. Thank you."

"It's my pleasure, Lady Gothel."

"I wonder what my sisters think of a Gorgon statue in our fountain?" she said, not meaning to say it aloud.

"I thought we should keep with the original themes for our new statuary and carvings. You don't like it?"

"No, Jacob, I love it. Please don't worry. I think it's beautiful. However, my sisters, especially Primrose, don't always share my aesthetic. Perhaps we can get some statues of frolicking dancers to surround the Gorgon? Something to make the tableau lighter. More lighthearted?"

"Yes, my little witch. As you wish," said Jacob as they made their way to the wagon.

Gothel gasped when she saw the wagon. It was laden with supplies and decorations for the winter solstice.

"I thought you would like it. I hoped you wouldn't mind I took it upon myself to order items for the winter solstice."

"No! Not at all. This is amazing. Primrose and Hazel will be so excited."

"I hoped that would be the case, my lady."

"This is incredible, Jacob. Maybe this will cheer them up! It's too bad the house won't be ready in time for the solstice."

"That is the other reason I wanted to speak with you. I think the house may be ready by the solstice."

"Really?" asked Gothel, truly excited for the first time in weeks.

"The foundation is sound, and the upper rooms are finished. We will be doing work downstairs for several more months, but there is no reason you can't move into your rooms, and decorate the morning room for the solstice."

"The morning room? It's finished?"

"Yes, Gothel."

"Can I see it?"

"Of course. Follow me."

Sir Jacob led Gothel into the house. It was strange; she had never imagined seeing the house this way, so airy and light, so open and filled with windows. There was a striking contrast between the renovated areas and the parts of the house that had not been destroyed in the confrontation with her mother. It was like walking the fine line between dreams and nightmares.

The rooms dominated by the stone carvings were like another world altogether. Gothel had never seen it that way before, not until she saw them in contrast to the new rooms. She imagined Primrose saying it was like waking up from a terrible dream. Yet somehow the old part of the house was even more beautiful in Gothel's eyes. The gargoyles perched on sconces didn't seem to be leering at her, but rather looking down at her protectively.

"Come this way, lady, I will show you the morning room."

It was exactly how Gothel had imagined it would look when she asked Jacob to have it built, filled with windows on every side, almost like a lighthouse. She was happy she had asked him to create that room for her sisters. A room with light. A room for celebrations, where they could make new memories so they could forget all the terrible things that had happened with their mother. The morning room was octagonal, and there were window seats in almost every nook. And in the center of the room was a massive winter solstice tree stretching up to the glass dome ceiling. Beside the tree were wooden crates bursting with decorations for Gothel and her sisters to put up. She saw little birds, shiny golden balls, silver stars, and red hearts made of glass. *Oh! Primrose is going to love those!*

"This is going to make my sisters so happy. Thank you, Sir Jacob. Thank you so much."

"Of course, my lady. I see no reason why you shouldn't move in straightaway."

"I agree! I can't wait to tell my sisters."

"I will leave you to that, then, lady, so I may get back to my other duties."

"Before you go, Jacob, I have question." But Jacob already knew what Gothel was going to ask him. And his answer was the same as it had been the countless times she had asked the question before.

"As I said before, my little witch, I haven't heard

anything from your mother. I do believe you successfully sent her to the mists."

"But how?" asked Gothel, her gray eyes wide.

"Only you can answer that, my little witch."

"That's the problem—I can't."

CHAPTER XIII

The Eve Before the Longest Night

The young witches were all moved into the main house and getting ready for the winter solstice. They inhabited most of the second floor but spent the majority of their time in the new morning room, the old library, and their bedrooms. Since the dining room was still under construction, they took most of their meals in the morning room. This day they were enjoying their breakfast while sitting in one of the window seats, their tea and biscuits before them on a little round table.

Since the confrontation with their mother, the dead woods hadn't been so dreary. Even with winter coming, the sky seemed less gray, and they sometimes even got sunlight in the morning room. They had a spectacular panoramic view of the dead woods, and they could see all the way to the thicket in every direction.

"I wonder when we will see the first snowfall," said Gothel. "Hazel, do you smell snow?"

"Not yet, Gothel. But soon."

They were preparing for the longest night. This year, Gothel had her own ideas of how to celebrate now that their mother wasn't there to dictate how they spent their holidays. Usually it was a somber affair, everyone in black and the main house entirely dark and freezing cold. Their mother wouldn't even allow fires in the hearths on the longest night. Manea welcomed the death of winter and celebrated the longest night with a day of fasting and the reciting of the names of all their ancestors while leaving them little gifts and offerings of their favorite foods on a communal alter. It was a somber version of Samhain, during which the lives of their ancestors were celebrated. Manea had little oval oil paintings of all their ancestors in wooden frames, which she set on the family altar, and she would tell the girls their stories in succession. After the stories, they would stand at the altar, looking at the portraits in silence, careful to stay perfectly still so as not to frighten away the ghosts of their ancestors should they decide to visit them on the longest night.

This year there will be a portrait of Mother among the others.

Her sisters didn't seem to be excited about the solstice even though Gothel had gone out of her way to make sure they'd enjoy themselves. Never once in their entire upbringing had their mother allowed them to have a solstice tree or exchange gifts, and Gothel thought having the tree would lighten her sisters' heavy hearts, but they still moped around the house, lackluster and peaky.

"We should decorate the solstice tree today, Primrose!" said Gothel as she smeared chocolate hazelnut spread on a biscuit, looking at the bare tree.

"If you wish, Gothel," said Primrose, yawning.

"What's wrong, Prim? Are you okay? Still not feeling well?"

"I'm just exhausted all the time. And honestly I'm not excited about the longest night."

"That's because I haven't told you how we're going to celebrate!"

"We're going to do what we do every year," said Hazel, picking at a biscuit.

Hazel had gotten frightfully thin the past few months, and her eyes looked weary. Both of Gothel's sisters looked pallid, actually. Gothel looked at them, wondering what she could do to liven their spirits.

"We're going to fill this entire house with light!"

"What?" asked Hazel and Primrose in unison.

"You heard me! Every single room will be filled with light! Look out the window! The wagons arrived this morning while you were sleeping!"

Primrose and Hazel went to windows that faced the courtyard. Sir Jacob was down there, directing their minions like a wizard performing magic on a windy hilltop, gesticulating and pointing in various directions with great fervor.

"Are those candles?"

"Yes! Wagons and wagons of them! We are

going to infuse this house with light! I've been reading about how other witches celebrate the longest night, and there are some witches who feel it's best to make it a celebration of light."

"Where did you read that?" asked Hazel.

"In one of the books that came in one of Jacob's many wagons."

"You've grown rather dependent upon him. Do you think that's wise?" asked Primrose.

"He's happy to have the work. He likes to be busy. Mother always kept him tucked away in his crypt unless she needed him for battle or to handle the deliveries."

"He never sleeps, Gothel! He's always awake, doing things for us!" said Hazel, making Gothel laugh.

"You're right, he never sleeps. And he'd rather have something to do than sit in his crypt, waiting to be called upon. I've talked to him about this already, Hazel. I promise this is what he'd prefer."

"And what about the minions? Do you let them rest?" Hazel asked.

"Hazel, we've gone over this so many times. He works them in shifts, letting them sleep for days at a time before they have to work again. And before you ask again, the children are not awake in their graves, they're sleeping." Gothel stood up and walked over to her sister. "Hazel, I'm worried about you. You keep forgetting things."

"I'm just tired, Gothel. I'm fine."

"You're getting so thin. Can you please eat, just a little bit? Isn't there something I can tempt you with? Is there something I can have Jacob fetch for you?"

"No, Gothel. I'm fine. I think I'll go to my room and lie down. I have a headache."

"Okay, Hazel, rest well."

Gothel watched nervously as her sister left the room. Never in their lives had any of them been ill. It just didn't happen. Gothel didn't know what to make of that. She decided she would spend the day in her mother's library and see if there was something she could do to help Hazel.

"Prim, I'm going to Mother's library. Do you

want to put some of those red hearts on the tree? I had them made for you."

"Yes, I think I will. Can you ask Jacob to send someone up to help with the boxes?"

"Really? I didn't think you'd want any of Mother's creatures in here."

"I feel a little differently now. Some of them were destroyed while protecting us from Mother. They're our creatures now."

"I'm happy you see it that way. I'll have Jacob send someone up to help you."

As Gothel made her way out of the morning room and down to her mother's private library, she ran into Jacob, who was supervising the renovations in the dining room.

"It's starting to come together in here," she said, looking around the room.

"Hello, Lady Gothel." Jacob always addressed her as such when they were around the other minions or her sisters. Otherwise he would call her "little witch," which she had started to find very endearing. Gothel honestly didn't know what she would do without him. "Lady, I had some questions for you about this room. You said you wanted shutters on these windows?"

Gothel was awestruck by the majesty of the room now. It still had its stone carvings of harpies and ravens in flight and its many large windows cut right out of the stone, but the minion workers had installed hinged windows so the room could still be open to the elements if they chose. It was brilliant the way they had done it, with the frames of the windows painted to match the stone, giving the room the illusion of looking as it had before. The contrast between the dark stone and the grayish-blue sky was remarkable. "I'm not so sure I do now."

"I thought you might feel differently. I hope you don't mind I had the windows fitted. It seemed a shame to shut out the view and the light."

"You're right. And I love the new table, chairs, rugs, and red tapestries. Oh! And the chandeliers and new wall sconces! Thank you, Jacob!"

"My pleasure," said Jacob, betraying some pride in his work.

"Jacob?"

"Yes?"

"Are you truly happy with all this work? Hazel and Primrose have been worried about you."

"I am quite happy, my little witch," said Jacob under his breath. "But I am worried about your sisters. I don't wish to alarm you, but I'm afraid your mother caused them permanent damage during the attack. I don't wish to overstep, little witch, but I think it's time to explore the situation."

"I was on my way to do just that. I'm heading down to Mother's private library now."

"It's your library now, lady. Don't forget that."

"Thank you, Jacob. I'll be there if you need me."

CHAPTER XIV

THE ODD SISTERS IN THE DEAD WOODS

Gothel had taken one of her books into the dense part of the woods near the city of the dead, just as she used to with her sisters in the days before she killed their mother. She wanted to be somewhere quiet away from the main house and the sound of the renovations. Her sisters were napping, but she had made sure to leave them their favorite pastries and fruit to try to tempt them to eat if they woke before she got back to the house.

She was lying on one of the empty graves, her back against a tombstone. The sun cast a pattern of light on the pages of her book through the dead weeping willow branches. She watched the patterns dance and change as the breeze swayed the branches, distracting her from her reading. She made it her custom to lie only on the graves of those who were at the house doing work. Now that she'd met many of her minions, it somehow felt disrespectful to disturb them while they were sleeping.

She was reading a book written by her mother on various remedies and counter spells. She was desperately worried about her sisters' health and hoped she could find something in one of the many books her mother had left behind. She had thought in the beginning they were just traumatized and exhausted by the entire ordeal with their mother, and to some extent she still thought that might be the case, but it had been several months and they weren't better. She had to admit there might be something terribly wrong with them, and she was determined to find out what it was.

Gothel had always been a quick study, but she knew she would never have the knowledge of her ancestors—not after the confrontation she'd had with her mother—so she figured she'd better read as many of her mother's books as she could. She had been to the vault where her mother's blood was kept only to get the gold coins Jacob needed for supplies. Now, with everything going on with her sisters, she wondered if she should just share the blood with them to save their lives. But she couldn't help thinking about the things her mother had said, about having to hide parts of herself from her sisters. If she gave them the blood, they would know her completely. Lately her sisters were always sleeping, and Gothel was pretty much left to herself to do as she wished. She had to admit she enjoyed having that freedom.

No, that doesn't mean you wish them dead, Gothel.

She daily had to will herself from thinking like her mother. She loved her sisters more than anything. She was sitting in the woods now poring over her mother's book, trying to find a cure for them, wasn't she? Though something told her the cure was likely in her mother's blood. But she couldn't shut out her mother's words warning her not to share it with her sisters. Warning her they would not like her if they could read her thoughts. She remembered her mother's prediction that Gothel was meant to be alone. But how could that be? She would always have Jacob. She would always have the minions. And if she could help it, she would always have her sisters. *Mother is the queen of lies.* She and her sisters were meant to be together.

Sisters. Together. Forever. That was their vow. *If I have to share Mother's blood, then so be it!*

Gothel slammed down her book, frustrated she had wasted the day trying to find a cure when she knew full well she would have to use her mother's blood. She didn't know how she knew; she just knew.

"You know because your mother's blood flows through you like a current."

Gothel looked up, startled. She quickly got to her feet and backed away from the three young women standing before her in the shadows of the dead weeping willows. They were wearing black dresses with elaborate brocade bodices stitched in silver. Their full skirts hit just below their knees and were trimmed with many layers of tiered lace, accenting their black-and-white striped stockings and shiny black pointed boots.

"Who in Hades are you and how did you get into my woods?" asked Gothel sternly.

"I am Lucinda, and these are my sisters Ruby and Martha. I'm sorry we frightened you," one of them said with a sweet smile.

Gothel took in the odd young women. They were about the same age as Gothel and her sisters, maybe a year or two older, surely not in their twenties yet. They were identical in every way, including the way they were dressed. They all had long thick black hair that hung in soft waves to their shoulders. Their skin was pale and was beautifully contrasted by their dark eyes and red lips. There was something about the girls that seemed familiar to her, but she couldn't put her finger on it.

"Of course we are familiar to you. We are all witches together," said the girl who called herself Lucinda.

Mind readers! thought Gothel, feeling panicked.

"Yes, we can read your thoughts. I'm sorry if that makes you uncomfortable. But I promise we don't mean you any harm. We're here to help you, actually. We felt your magic in the world when you destroyed the queen of the dead, and we felt your distress. It reached well beyond the many kingdoms to our lands, and we couldn't help coming to your aid. We want to help you heal your sisters."

"Heal my sisters? How did you know?" asked Gothel. "Why would you want to do that for someone you don't know?" She was not at all convinced the strange sisters were there to help.

"So many questions," said Ruby, laughing.

"We are all witches together. We need to watch out for each other. Help each other," said Lucinda.

"And what would you want in return?" asked Gothel, eyeing the sisters.

"We would like access to your mother's books. We specifically would like to learn the arts of necromancy and the secrets of your ancestors' long lives," said Lucinda, smiling.

"You're asking for quite a bit," said Gothel.

"I'd say any price was worth saving your sisters," said Martha, though it might have been any one of them saying it. Their voices were all the same.

Martha walked over to Gothel, offering her hand. "I promise you we are here to help. If you don't want to share your mother's books, we will still help you. It's no matter to us. You asked what we would like, and that is what we would like. But it's not a requirement. We will help you nevertheless."

"Oh yes! We will help you no matter! I could never imagine what it would be like to lose my sisters. I promise we will do all we can to help you, Gothel," said Lucinda.

"Yes! We promise!" said Ruby.

Gothel's head spun as she listened to the sisters talk in succession. She didn't know what to make of the girls. She had never met other witches before, aside from her own family, and she found it a bit overwhelming to meet so many at once. She realized then how very isolated she had been, living in her own world with no one but her family and minions.

"Wait! How did you get through the thicket?"

asked Gothel, wondering how they had broken through her mother's enchantment.

The odd sisters looked at each other. "We have our ways."

Gothel was envious of the witches. They were clearly in possession of more magic than she could imagine or possibly wield.

"Do you think you could teach me how to use my magic?" Gothel asked.

The odd sisters laughed. "Of course we will, little witch. It would be our pleasure." That filled Gothel's heart with joy. She had finally found witches who could help her learn magic. Witches who promised to help her heal her sisters.

Gothel took Martha's hand and then took Lucinda's and Ruby's, grasping them together in hers. "Would you like to join us for the longest night, and for the solstice? We are having a festival of lights."

"The festival of lights in the dead woods? I don't think that has ever happened in anyone's lifetime. I wouldn't want to miss that," said Ruby.

"Of course we will join you for the solstice! It would be our honor!" said Lucinda.

"Shall I show you to the house, then? Sir Jacob will be there, getting everything ready for this evening. I can show you to your guest room, where you can refresh yourselves before the festival."

"Thank you," said the mysterious beauties with one voice, like a choir of sirens.

"Ah, and I should mention something about Sir Jacob. Well, you see, he—"

"We know all about Sir Jacob. Don't worry," said Lucinda, interrupting Gothel.

"How do you know about him?" asked Gothel.

"We saw him in your mind when you mentioned his name. We saw the image you hold of him in your mind," said Martha, smiling.

"I see."

"Of course we expected necromantic servants in the dead woods," Lucinda said.

"Yes. Of course you did."

Gothel felt out of her depth with the witches. She was interested in seeing what Hazel made of them, whether she would be able to tell if they had good intentions.

"Come this way," she said as they walked the long path that led them to the new courtyard, which was now filled with beautiful statues surrounding a large fountain. In the center of the fountain was the massive statue of a striking Gorgon. She had a wide evil grin with sharp teeth and wild curling snakes for hair. Her large stone eyes somehow sparked with life. She looked pleased, the stone Gorgon, as if she had just turned the frolicking dancers that surrounded her into stone, and it seemed to Gothel that during the Gorgon's height of glee, she perhaps caught a glimpse of her own reflection in the water, turning herself into stone as well. Gothel wondered what her sisters made of the new fountain. She wondered if they found it beautiful, like she did. She talked with her sisters very little those days; she was so busy trying to make the house beautiful for them that she somehow managed to neglect them.

"And don't forget your magic. You've been studying your mother's magic, trying to find a cure to help them," said Lucinda, reading Gothel's mind.

"Yes. That's true." Gothel wasn't sure she liked having mind readers about. Now she understood why the thought of mind reading unnerved Primrose.

"We look forward to meeting your sisters," said Lucinda as they reached the vestibule, which was still under construction. Sir Jacob was there, directing the minions like a great general at war.

"Sir Jacob, I would like to introduce Lucinda, Ruby, and Martha. They will be our guests for the longest night and the solstice."

Jacob stood for a moment saying nothing. Gothel didn't know if it was from the shock of seeing strangers in the dead wood, or if it was something else. Whatever his reasons, he looked unsettled.

"Welcome, ladies. Please let Lady Gothel know if there is anything I can do to make your stay more comfortable," he said, eyeing the sisters, his face strained but not from the twisted smile Gothel had grown so fond of.

"Thank you, Sir Jacob," said the girls in unison. It was almost like a song the way they said it.

Gothel wondered if this was the way she and her sisters would be if they were identical, and if her mother would have been happier if these had been her daughters rather than Gothel and her sisters. Would she have tried to kill them if they had been identical, like these girls? Her mother's voice echoed in her mind.

Indistinguishable witch daughters are a blessing from the gods.

Had her mother ever said anything kind to them? Gothel couldn't recall any encouragement from her mother—not until the days preceding her death. But now she was almost sure everything her mother had said in those days was a lie. She felt foolish for believing that her mother would be anything but traitorous.

"Don't discount everything your mother said to you in those final days, Gothel. Not all of it was lies."

Gothel looked at Lucinda with a blank face. She needed to remember those girls could hear all her thoughts.

"We can teach you how to block people from hearing your thoughts," said Ruby.

"No offense, but I think I would like that very much." Gothel realized she had been rude to poor Jacob, who had been standing there the entire time, almost mesmerized by the sisters. Almost afraid. Maybe that wasn't the right word: *afraid*. But clearly there was something about the sisters that bothered him. She would have to talk with him later when the sisters were occupied in their rooms.

"Thank you, Jacob. I won't keep you from your work. I will come see you later before we start the longest night."

"Yes, Lady Gothel." And he went on his way, directing the minions to finish putting up the decorations and setting up the candles around the house.

The strange sisters laughed. Gothel liked the sound of their laughter. It wasn't teasing or nasty; it was musical and happy. She missed laughing with her sisters that way. She missed spending time with them.

"We'll do what we can to help your sisters. We promise," said Martha.

"Thank you," said Gothel. "Let me show you to your rooms."

"We prefer to stay in the same room if it's all the same," said Lucinda.

"Yes, of course. We'll put you in the dragon room, then. It has the largest bed—that is, if you don't mind sharing," Gothel said, directing them up the stairs.

"We don't mind," said the smiling sisters, looking around the mansion, their little boots clicking on the stone floors. *Click click click.* The sound was starting to annoy Gothel, making her head slightly spin. She laughed to herself. *At least I will always know when they're coming.*

The sisters joined in Gothel's laughter. Gothel didn't bother responding. She pretended they didn't hear her thoughts as they made their way up the stairs and past the skeleton creatures that were placing candles on every surface. There were candles everywhere, on every available space.

"Your room is this way," said Gothel, pointing to a large stone archway. The dragon room was in the oldest part of the house, and it was one of their grandest rooms. Gothel always wondered why her mother had never stayed in that room herself. It was the best of all the bedrooms, with its stone carvings of dragons stretching across its walls, and the giant fireplace flanked with the winged beasts.

"She didn't want to live in the room where her mother died," said Lucinda.

Gothel was startled. The words were like a knife in her stomach, and she knew there must be truth to them. It hurt her to think the girls knew something about her mother that she did not.

"How do you know this?" asked Gothel, eyeing Lucinda.

"The many queens of the dead are legendary. Their histories are written in the volumes of time, which we have read voraciously."

"You probably know more about my history than I do," said Gothel, distracted, as she watched a couple of skeleton minions opening the curtains and starting a fire. Never in the time of her mother had there been so many servants roaming the house. At least not that she and her sisters witnessed. She smiled, realizing she had become her own queen after all. She was doing things her own way.

"I hope you will enjoy your stay with us. You're welcome to stay as long as you wish. I will have someone bring up a number of dresses and everything else you might need. You look to be the same size as my sister Hazel, and we just got a delivery containing more dresses and nightclothes than she could possibly wear in her lifetime."

"Thank you, Gothel. Or should we call you Queen?"

Gothel laughed. "I'm certainly not your queen. Gothel is fine. Thank you." She motioned to the stone desk, which held a large blotter, a bottle of ink, and a feather quill. "There is paper in the drawer if you need to write your family to let them know you're staying. And if there is anything you need, please let one of my creatures know. They can arrange a bath, bring you something to eat, anything you require. None of them speak, of course, other than Jacob, but they can hear and understand you."

"Thank you, Gothel," said the sisters, seemingly awestruck as they looked around the room. Gothel suddenly saw it through their eyes, that room she had taken for granted until that moment, its massive feather bed nestled on the large carved-stone bed frame with its four posts, the tops of which were fashioned in the shapes of dragon heads. The red canopy and bed drapes were new additions to the room since her mother's passing, as were the crimson tapestries and rugs. It was a striking room, and she wondered why she hadn't taken it for herself.

"Well, you should! After we leave, of course!" said Martha, laughing.

"Oh yes, before I forget . . ." said Gothel. "Someone will come get you before nightfall and bring you to the morning room for the celebration. Jacob will ring the dressing bell two hours before the festivities. In the meantime, please be sure to ring the bell if you need anything at all. Now, if you will excuse me, I would like to go check in on my sisters."

"Of course," said the witches.

Gothel left the room, closing the door behind her. She could hear the witches laughing as she walked down the hall toward her sisters' rooms.

What peculiar, odd sisters.

CHAPTER XV

THE LONGEST NIGHT

All six of the witches stood silently in the court-yard, waiting for Sir Jacob to come down from the house. Gothel had thought they would all be meeting in the morning room, but it seemed Sir Jacob had other plans.

Hazel, Gothel, and Primrose were wearing lovely dresses Gothel had recently picked out for them for the solstice. They were black, in keeping with their mother's tradition, but they were speckled with a cascade of embroidered silver stars that swirled down from their right shoulders, twisting around the bodice and then becoming more spread out, like the night sky, when the stars reached their

voluminous skirts. All three of the girls had decorated their hair with glittering stars.

Lucinda, Ruby, and Martha had elected to wear
the dresses they had arrived in. When Gothel looked
more closely, she realized the silver embroidery on
their bodices was in little star patterns. Though
they hadn't changed their dresses, the odd sisters
had arranged their hair in elaborate buns worn high
on their heads, with long ringlets that hung on
both sides of their faces. Their buns were adorned
with silver stars that matched their earrings and the
magnificent necklaces Gothel had sent up to their
rooms as solstice gifts. All six of them were bundled
in white fur wraps and muffs to protect them from
the cold.

The purple twilight sky was starting to darken
to the color of eggplants, and there was the stillness
in the air that always told Gothel it was about to
snow. She could feel the chill kissing her cheeks,
likely turning them a rosy color like her sisters'. She
could see their breath. To Gothel they all seemed
like dragon witches, breathing smoke as they waited.

"Will it be much longer, Gothel?" asked Primrose, clearly becoming impatient.

"I'm not sure, Prim. Oh wait, look. There he is."

In the distance, they saw Jacob making his way down from the main house. He was carrying a torch, illuminating his skull-like features.

"Good evening, young witches. So sorry to keep you waiting," said Jacob when he finally got to the courtyard. "Since this is my ladies' first winter solstice during their reign as queens, I wanted to make the longest night an even more special occasion." Gothel saw Jacob eyeing their guests. She hadn't had the opportunity to speak with him privately on the matter, and she was even more curious now what he thought about the witches.

"I present, for the very first time in our lands, the festival of lights!" Jacob raised his torch, signaling Victor, who was watching from the house, and within moments the entire house and its grounds were filled with the most magnificent light Gothel and her sisters had ever seen.

"Oh, Jacob! It's remarkable! Thank you," said Gothel, smiling at her sisters' happy faces.

"It's my pleasure, my queen," said Jacob, gesturing for all the witches to follow him. "Come, my ladies. Come out of the cold. Queen Gothel has arranged a magnificent feast for the celebration."

"Oh, Gothel, a feast?" asked Primrose, smiling.

"The house is so beautiful, Gothel! Thank you!" said Hazel.

Gothel loved seeing her sisters so happy. "I wanted our first celebration together without Mother to be special! I wanted to make you happy! Please tell me you're happy!" But they didn't have to answer: within moments she was enveloped in her sisters' embraces.

"Thank you, Gothel!" they squealed. "Thank you!"

"Yes, it's very beautiful," said the odd sisters, mesmerized by the lights from the house. The morning room looked especially brilliant from a distance. "That room there, it reminds us of the Lighthouse of the Gods."

"Thank you! That was my intention."

"Oh, you've been there?" asked Lucinda as they all followed Jacob through the vestibule and up the stairs leading them to the morning room.

"No, I've only read about it. We've never left the dead woods," said Gothel sadly as they entered the morning room. There were hundreds of skeletons quietly making their way out of the house and back to their graves. It became clear that Jacob had arranged for them all to light the candles at once. There wasn't a surface that wasn't covered in candles. The house was entirely filled with light, the way Gothel had imagined. As they entered the morning room, she was struck by the beauty of the solstice tree placed in the center, stretching to the top of the glass dome overhead. The tree was covered in red glass hearts, birds, and glittering glass balls of various colors that sparkled in the candlelight.

At the far end of the room was an altar with the small oil paintings of their ancestors, and in the center was a portrait of their mother. There were hazelnuts, tea, oranges, various flowers, and chocolates on the table, as well as a brass bell and a pretty teacup they only brought out for that occasion. The teacup was silver with black skulls, and it had a chip with a hairline crack. There were also an emerald broach, a remarkably beautiful diamond necklace, a string of pearls, and an onyx ring—all possessions of their ancestors, all treasures their mother had kept in a wooden box in the vault and brought out for that occasion. The altar was filled with many taper candles of different heights in silver candlestick holders. Those candles seemed to burn more brightly than the others; the light was almost blinding, which had been Gothel's intent. She didn't want her sisters to have to see their mother's portrait if they didn't want to. She would have done away with the altar altogether for that celebration, but she didn't want to anger her ancestors any more than necessary. She was already afraid they would be offended the witches were not celebrating the longest night under the cover of dark, in solemn contemplation.

Under the tree was a pile of gifts wrapped in red and silver paper, with black bows and little white tags. There were even gifts under the tree for their guests. It had all been seen to by Jacob, who wanted to be sure that no one was left out of the festivities. Gothel was astounded by Jacob's attention to detail and had to admit she was utterly dependent upon him.

"Now, if you ladies would like to follow me to the dining room, dinner is ready," said Jacob.

The dining room had a blazing fire in the fireplace, casting light and shadows on the harpies carved into the stone wall. The room was warm even with the windows open to reveal a spectacular view of the courtyard that had replaced the conservatory.

"It's so lovely in here, Jacob, thank you."

"Come to the windows. I have something to show you," he said to all the witches.

Gothel could see just beyond the courtyard, in a small greenhouse near the carriage house, the light of the rapunzel flower, amplified by the greenhouse windows. She had almost forgotten it existed, with all the renovations and vexation about her sisters' health. She wondered if the visiting witches knew what that one tiny light was. She started to become nervous. She hadn't thought what it meant to have other witches in her home and on her grounds so near the flower. Did they think it was a candle for the festival of lights, or did they know the flower was their secret?

Jacob could see that Gothel was concerned, which in turn concerned him. But within moments other lights started to appear in the courtyard. That, not the flower, was the surprise he had intended to share with his witches. Each one of the formerly frolicking stone dancers near the fountain was now holding glowing candles in its stone hands, and in the center of the fountain was the Gorgon, surrounded by floating candles illuminating her gleeful grin. It was a beautiful spectacle. And then, one by one, lights started to appear throughout the woods. Thousands of candles lit up the entire forest, all held in the hands of her devoted minions. It was remarkable, not only the brilliance, but this show of power to her guests. It was like an endless sea of light that stretched out as far as they could see.

"Thank you, Jacob. Thank you for everything you have done for us this night, and every other since the passing of our mother," said Gothel sincerely.

"It's my pleasure, my queen." Gothel noticed Jacob had been referring to her as his queen since the arrival of the odd witches. She was almost eager to get the evening over with so she would have the opportunity to talk with him alone. "Please, everyone, take your seats. Dinner will get cold," said Jacob, directing the witches to their chairs.

The witches took their seats at the long wooden table, which was covered in a bounty of delicious foods and tiny votive candles in glass holders. Jacob managed to include everyone's favorites, even those of the odd sisters, who helped themselves to large portions of baked apples spiced with brown sugar and cinnamon and served with cold cream.

"How did you know we loved cherries in brandy?" asked Ruby as she poured them over a hearty piece of walnut cake.

"Jacob is a master at anticipating our every whim," said Gothel, smiling at her guests.

To Gothel's surprise, Primrose and Hazel piled their plates high with their favorites, as well. Primrose was munching on cherry tarts, while Hazel was spreading chocolate hazelnut butter on thinly grilled cakes covered with a light dusting of powdered sugar. Gothel thought she would happily provide her sisters with a feast every day if it meant she would be able to get them to eat. Maybe it was the warmness of the room, but it seemed to Gothel her sisters had more color in their cheeks. The evening was everything she wanted it to be.

Between taking bites of her tart and sipping wine, Primrose was asking the new witches a litany of questions.

"How long have you been studying magic? Where do you live? How did you find us in the dead woods? How does your magic work?" And on she went, not even giving the witches time to answer. It was nice to see Primrose so happy and so full of life. *Like her old self,* Gothel thought. Hazel was quiet, as was her custom. She was the contemplative sister. The observer. She let Primrose, the outgoing sister, ask all the questions and sat there listening carefully to the responses.

"Give them a chance to answer, Prim!" said Gothel, laughing.

"That's okay, Gothel. We understand," said Martha. "We felt the same way when we met other witches for the first time. But it must be even more overwhelming for you after being here alone for so many years."

"It is!" said Primrose. "We've had no one here in the dead woods our entire lives. Imagine living your entire life not meeting a soul other than your sisters and mother. And Jacob, of course." She looked at Jacob, standing nearby in case anyone required anything. "Jacob! Why aren't you joining us?" she asked. If Jacob could have blushed, he would have. Gothel could tell he was touched by Primrose's gesture.

"Thank you, Lady Primrose, but I should check in on the kitchen. Since you ladies seem to be favoring the sweets rather than the savory dishes, I think I will request the other desserts be brought out immediately."

"Oh!" squealed Primrose. "That sounds lovely!"

The odd sisters laughed. "Is it always like this? So happy? We hadn't expected to see such a happy group of witches when we decided to venture here."

Hazel spoke. "I mean no offense, but why do you ask questions when you already know the answers?"

The witch sisters smiled at Hazel. "Ah. We thought you were the empathetic one," said Lucinda.

"How so?" asked Hazel, speaking up more than was usual for her.

"We were hoping the three of you could read minds," said Ruby. "It makes things so much easier when getting to know new witches if we can just read each other's minds."

"Wait, you can read minds?" asked Primrose.

The odd sisters laughed. "Yes," they said.

Primrose frowned.

The odd sisters laughed again. "I wouldn't worry about it, Primrose," said Lucinda. "You have such a pure heart, and you are so kind, you really have nothing to hide."

"I like these girls!" said Primrose, smiling at her own sisters. "I think we should keep them!"

"I am curious," said Hazel, "how it was you were able to enter our woods. Our mother always told us the boundary was enchanted."

"And so it is, but we devised a counter spell that allowed us to enter. We didn't think you'd mind," Lucinda said, taking Hazel's measure.

"That's rather audacious," said Hazel.

"It is audacious! And I like it!" Primrose said, smiling, then laughing.

"Yes, of course you would," said Hazel.

"I'm sorry if we overstepped, Hazel. I thought we were welcome," said Lucinda.

"You are welcome," said Primrose. "I think what Hazel was trying to say is that she is impressed with your magic."

"Is that what you're trying to say, Hazel?" Ruby asked.

"As a matter of fact, it is," said Hazel. "You'll have to excuse me, ladies. We're not used to visitors here, and I'm afraid I don't share my sister's flair for entertaining. I'm not quite as charming as my other sisters here." She returned her attention to her meal.

"Please, don't apologize, Hazel. We are honored to be here," said Lucinda, raising her glass. "To the witches of the dead woods!"

"To the witches of the dead woods!" said the other witches, laughing and clinking their glasses.

After another hour or so of chatting over dessert, the ladies moved the party into the morning room. Several more trays of desserts, tea, and coffee were on a rolling cart near one of the larger window seats, where all the ladies made themselves comfortable. Each set of sisters found themselves seated across from the others.

"Sisters," said Gothel, talking to her own sisters, "I have told Lucinda, Ruby, and Martha they may stay as long as they wish. And depending on how you feel about this, I would like to give them access to Mother's books. They have agreed to help us learn our magic."

"Oh! I think that's a lovely idea," said Primrose. Gothel was surprised. "I know how important magic is to you, Gothel, and I'd much rather have these lovely creatures teach you than Mother." Primrose looked at Hazel and asked, "What do you think, Hazel?"

Hazel contemplated the witches carefully before answering. "I think that is a very fine idea, but I have a feeling Gothel isn't being entirely honest with us."

Gothel's heart sank. She didn't know what Hazel was talking about. Lucinda smiled and answered for her. "You're right, Hazel. We didn't want to mention it and put a damper on the festivities, but we are here for another reason. We want to help you and Primrose. Gothel has been worried about you—so worried, in fact, that she unintentionally called us here. You see, we can feel magic in the world. And we felt Gothel's when she destroyed your mother."

"But I don't even know how I did it! I still don't think it was my magic," said Gothel.

"Well, we're here to help you figure that out," said Martha.

"Why are you worried about me and Hazel?" asked Primrose.

Gothel had a feeling Primrose didn't realize how sick she likely was. "Because, Prim, you two haven't been yourselves since Mother attacked you. We're worried she's caused some kind of irreparable harm."

"We're just tired, Gothel. I think you're making more of this than is necessary."

"Prim, it's been months and you're not getting better!" Gothel hadn't meant to raise her voice, but she sometimes found Primrose's Hades-may-care attitude annoying.

"I think you're being dramatic, Gothel. As usual!"

"No, Prim, Gothel is right. There is something terribly wrong with us. I didn't want to frighten you, but I think we should do something about it as soon as we can manage."

"Really? Do you think it's that bad?" asked Primrose. But before one of her own sisters could answer, Martha chimed in.

"Don't worry, Primrose, my sisters and I will help you. I promise. Your mother lived an extraordinarily long life. Somewhere deep within one of her books will be the answer. I promise you."

"I'm so glad you're here," said Primrose to the odd sisters.

"We all are," said Gothel.

"Yes, very glad indeed," said Hazel.

"Now, shall we open our gifts before the evening takes a darker turn?" asked Gothel, trying to lighten the mood. The truth was she was very worried about her sisters—even more now that Hazel had admitted she agreed something was wrong—but she didn't want to worry Primrose any more than needed.

She just hoped the odd sisters would be able to help her save Primrose and Hazel.

CHAPTER XVI

JACOB'S MISGIVINGS

Lucinda and her sisters hadn't come down for breakfast yet, and Gothel's sisters were sleeping in, as they often did. Gothel told Jacob not to have them disturbed, to let them sleep as long as they wished. They had all stayed up quite late the night before, opening gifts. But Gothel had gotten up early. She wanted the opportunity to talk with Jacob alone in the quiet of early morning, when the light was still a muted blue.

She found him at the little greenhouse talking with a number of skeletal creatures about something that seemed rather important.

"Good morning, Jacob."

"Good morning, little witch."

"What's going on here?" she asked, wondering if something was wrong.

"Just taking some security measures."

"Jacob, may I speak with you privately?"

"It's safe to talk in front of your minions, little witch."

"I can tell there is something bothering you about our guests. I'd like to know what it is."

"Yes. I was planning to come to you after I was done here. I think it would be best if you sent those sisters away at once. Your mother foresaw the destruction of this place many years ago, and she saw it in the form of three witches."

"That could have been me and my sisters, Jacob. I destroyed the rapunzel, and I killed our mother, almost destroying the entire dead woods in the process. I fulfilled the prophecy myself."

"She always said it would be three witches wearing the same face."

"Perhaps she was wrong, Jacob. Maybe she didn't see correctly."

"Your mother's visions were rarely wrong. Please trust me, Gothel. I don't trust these witches. You don't know anything about them. Where they're from, why they're really here. For all you know, they are here to steal the rapunzel. They could be here to take your place as queen! You've never met witches before, Gothel. They are wicked, horrid creatures, envious of each other's powers, greedy for more magic. Why did they say they came?"

"To help Primrose and Hazel."

"And in exchange?" he asked, startling Gothel with how informal he was being with her.

"They want to know Mother's magic. They want to learn how to raise the dead, and how Mother was able to live so long."

"Then they do want the flower."

Why is he worried about the flower? Gothel wondered. It wasn't the flower that animated him—if it were, he would be fully flesh, like a living being. "Don't worry, Jacob—you will not be harmed if the rapunzel is gone. That is another kind of magic. I spoke with Mother about it briefly. The flower—"

"I know all of this, Gothel. I am older than you are, I spent countless nights talking with your mother until the sun rose to greet us." Jacob paused. "Listen to me, these witches are not here to help, and even if they think they are, something horrible will happen. You have two choices, Gothel: either give your sisters the blood, or let them die. But whatever you do, take the blood yourself, because you can't truly rule here as queen until you do."

"You called me your queen last night."

"I wanted your guests to respect your station. But I am sure even they know you've not taken the blood. If you had, you wouldn't be asking them for their help with magic."

"But don't you see . . . if they don't show me how to use Mother's magic, who will? I need them!"

"Now listen to me, little one. This is important. Whatever you decide, do not let those witches anywhere near the blood or the flower. I don't care if your sisters' lives depend upon it. If you can't save your sisters on your own, then their lives were not meant to be. I'm sorry to say it, but these witches are not to be trusted. They're not your friends."

Gothel stood there, gobsmacked. She didn't have the proper words. She loved and respected Jacob, but she thought he was wrong.

"I hope you are wrong, Jacob."

"For your sake, I hope I am."

Chapter XVII

Blood and Flowers

It had been several weeks since the solstice, and the strange sisters were still in the dead woods. Jacob kept his reservations to himself, and Gothel kept him busy so she wouldn't have to see his disapproving looks and the worry on his face. She was convinced it was she her mother had seen in her vision and these witches were the only way she was going to be able to save her sisters.

Hazel and Primrose had now taken to their beds. They were weak and in constant pain. Gothel couldn't stand to see them that way and hid herself away in her mother's library with Lucinda and Ruby, desperately trying to find a way to save them.

Martha stayed with Hazel and Primrose, doing everything she could to make them more comfortable. She brewed them a daily poppy flower tea to manage their pain. She had offered to put them into a deep magical sleep, but Gothel was fearful that if their condition changed while they were sleeping, she wouldn't know.

"I can send them to the land of dreams, Gothel. They will be happy there, content and no longer in pain," Martha had said with sad eyes.

"But they wouldn't be able to tell me if they needed me! Please don't send them away," Gothel said. She could see the heartbreak on Martha's face.

"I understand. I will brew a powerful tea to keep them calm and without pain. It's made from the seeds of poppies. I promise it will not harm them." She touched Gothel's hand tenderly.

"Yes, please do that." Gothel felt helpless but, thankfully, not so alone with the odd sisters there to help her.

Gothel played the conversation she'd had with Martha again and again in her mind, wondering if she had made the right decision to keep Primrose and Hazel sedated rather than put in a magical trance, as she pored over her mother's books, desperately trying to find a way to save them.

"Gothel, please stop torturing yourself," said Lucinda, reading both Manea's book of the dead and Gothel's mind.

"What's that you're reading?" asked Gothel.

"Nothing that will help us, I'm afraid," said Lucinda, putting down the book in the pile designated as useless to their cause. "May I ask you a question? Why don't you want to give your sisters your mother's blood?"

"They don't want it! Especially Primrose."

"At this point I don't think she has a choice if she wants to live," Lucinda said, giving Gothel a sad look.

"It feels like I would be forcing something on her she doesn't want. But I can't stand by and watch her die."

"That is exactly what we are doing. We are on a deathwatch, Gothel. Whatever your reasons for not wanting to use your mother's blood, you need to make a choice. Either use your mother's blood or your sisters die."

"I think you're right. I really wanted to find another way, but it doesn't look like we will. I feel terrible we didn't use the blood sooner. But honestly, I'm afraid, Lucinda. I'm afraid of what will happen to us once we take her blood. And not just because my sisters will know my thoughts, but because I'm worried I will become more like my mother and I will lose my sisters forever."

"You will definitely lose them forever if you do not use your mother's blood," said Lucinda.

Gothel sighed. "Keep looking. We need to find the blood ritual."

"I have it right here, Gothel," said Lucinda.

"Thank you. I'll be right back."

Gothel stood at the door of her sisters' room. *My beautiful sleeping sisters.*

Martha heard Gothel's thoughts. "They are beautiful. I will give you some time alone with them. Where's Lucinda?"

"She's in the library," said Gothel, not taking her eyes off her sleeping sisters.

"I'll go find her," said Martha, patting Gothel on the shoulder.

Gothel quietly walked over to her sisters. She didn't want to wake them, but she wanted nothing more than to see their eyes. She just stood there, looking at them and wondering if they would be okay. Wondering if they would ever forgive her for giving them their mother's blood against their will. And like magic, Hazel opened her eyes and said, "Gothel, I love you." She held out her hand. "Take my hand, Sister."

Gothel took her sister's hand. "What is it?" she asked, tears running down her face.

"I trust you, Gothel. I want you to know that."

Gothel couldn't help bursting into tears. She sobbed and sobbed. "Thank you, Hazel. I hope Primrose will be able to forgive me."

Hazel smiled weakly, drifting back to sleep. "Don't worry. She will."

Gothel hoped Hazel was right. "Sleep now, my sister. I love you." But Hazel was asleep.

Gothel met with Lucinda, Ruby, and Martha in the hallway on her way down to the vault. "Can you sit with my sisters until I come back?"

"Of course. It will be our pleasure," said Lucinda.

As she was about to open the vault door with the large skeleton key, she was overcome by an inexplicable feeling that her mother was waiting for her in the vault. *Don't be so ridiculous, Gothel!* she told herself. Maybe it was just her mother's blood she was sensing. Maybe it was nothing at all, but she couldn't shake it. She had been standing there for what seemed like hours before she finally opened the door.

There was nothing there but wooden chests with her family's fortune. They had more money than they could need for many lifetimes over. But she supposed that was the point. Her family members lived extremely long lives.

Focus, Gothel. Find the blood.

She counted from the ceiling, like Jacob had instructed her, and pushed the seventh stone. There was a resounding sigh as a stone drawer sprung out of the wall, knocking her in the chest. It was as if her mother was giving her one final blow. But that wouldn't be the final blow, would it? Not if her sisters died.

"Stop it, Gothel!" she said aloud to no one but herself. "Your sisters are not going to die!"

Her mother's blood was in the drawer, as promised. It was in a glass bottle sealed with a waxed cork. Along with it was a note. Gothel's hands shook and her heart sank as she read it. She couldn't bear to see her mother's handwriting. It was fancy script, and old-fashioned, the capital letters large and ornate. It was addressed to her.

My dearest Gothel,

If you are reading this, then I have passed into the mists without giving you my blood. It is likely your instinct is to share the blood with your sisters, but this blood is meant for you alone.

If your sisters should ever fall ill,

the only thing that will help them is the
rapunzel flower. Take your sisters to the
conservatory amongst the flowers and
recite this incantation.

Flower, gleam and glow
Let your power shine
Make the clock reverse
Bring back what once was mine

Heal what has been hurt
Change the fates' design
Save what has been lost
Bring back what once was mine . . .

What once was mine

As the flowers glow, your sisters will be
restored. Keep reciting the incantation until

they are fully healed. This is your most important magic, Gothel. This is how you will stay young as long as you wish.

Protect the flower, my blackhearted daughter, until you are ready to meet me and your ancestors in the mists.

Mother

Gothel ran out of the vault, slamming the door behind her and forgetting to lock it. She ran up the stairs as fast as she could, but before she got to her sisters' bedroom, she met Lucinda, coming down the stairs to find her. "Oh, Gothel, I am so sorry." Lucinda was crying. She took Gothel's hand and led her to her Hazel and Primrose's room, where she found Ruby and Martha with wet blotchy faces. They were crying over her sisters.

"What happened?" Gothel asked, but she could see for herself what had happened. Her sisters had died. They had died while she was musing in the vault. They had died because she had taken too long.

"We're so sorry, Gothel. Lucinda was coming to get you!" said Martha, crying.

"What happened?" asked Gothel again, running to her sisters' bedside.

"I don't know! They just suddenly stopped breathing!" Martha said, clearly heartbroken.

"Jacob! Jacob!" Gothel screamed. She ran to the fireplace and pulled the lever that rang the bell for someone to come.

"Let me go find him," said Lucinda, running out of the room. "I will find him, don't worry!"

"Tell him to bring some others. We need to get my sisters to the greenhouse now!"

Gothel paced around the room, her heart pounding. "They can't die! They can't die. Oh please, don't let them die. This is all my fault."

Ruby and Martha went to Gothel and wrapped their arms around her, trying to calm her. "Shhh, Gothel, it will be okay."

Soon Jacob and his minions crowded into the room. "Jacob! Take my sisters down to the greenhouse, quickly."

Everyone in the room could see Jacob didn't think that would work, but he followed his queen's instructions. The minions took Primrose's and Hazel's bodies into their arms gently and carried them down the stairs, spiriting them away to the greenhouse.

"Jacob, please be careful! Don't hurt them!"

Gothel and the odd sisters followed the skeletal creatures out of the house, through the courtyard, and into the greenhouse. The greenhouse wasn't as large as the conservatory had been, but it was a beautifully built structure, with paned glass windows and a hinged ceiling that could be opened to let in the elements when desired. The skeletons stood there, wondering where Gothel wanted her sisters. "Put them there, on the ground next to the flower!" said Gothel.

"What can I do?" asked Jacob after the skeletons followed Gothel's orders.

"Nothing, just give me some room," Gothel replied.

She took out the crumpled letter she had shoved

into her pocket. Her hands were shaking, and her voice quivered as she recited her mother's incantation.

Flower, gleam and glow
Let your power shine
Make the clock reverse
Bring back what once was mine

Heal what has been hurt
Change the fates' design
Save what has been lost
Bring back what once was mine . . .

What once was mine

The flower glowed brighter as Gothel said the words, but her sisters remained the same.

Flower, gleam and glow
Let your power shine
Make the clock reverse
Bring back what once was mine

Heal what has been hurt
Change the fates' design
Save what has been lost
Bring back what once was mine . . .

What once was mine

Nothing happened. Gothel panicked. She didn't know what to do.

"Mother said this would work! She said it would heal them!"

"I don't think one flower alone is enough, Gothel," said Jacob, looking utterly helpless, his heart breaking for his queen.

"Let us say it with you, Gothel, maybe our magic can help!" said Lucinda.

"Oh yes! Please!" Gothel and the odd sisters said the incantation again, their voices in a fevered pitch and desperate.

Flower, gleam and glow
Let your power shine

Make the clock reverse
Bring back what once was mine

Heal what has been hurt
Change the fates' design
Save what has been lost
Bring back what once was mine . . .

What once was mine

Nothing. "Say it again!" screamed Gothel.

Lucinda looked at her sisters as if to say what they were doing was useless, but they said the words again, this time gathering all their power and sending their call into the many kingdoms and beyond in hopes that other witches in the world would send their power as well to help this poor little witch who was losing her precious sisters.

Flower, gleam and glow
Let your power shine
Make the clock reverse
Bring back what once was mine

Heal what has been hurt
Change the fates' design
Save what has been lost
Bring back what once was mine . . .

What once was mine

Then, suddenly, Hazel's and Primrose's bodies started to convulse. Their eyes opened briefly, locking their gazes on Gothel. "Please, let us die!" said Primrose before her eyes rolled back in her head and her body violently shook.

"Say it again!" Gothel screamed. "We have to save them!"

They said the words again as Gothel's sisters' bodies thrashed on the greenhouse floor. It was a grotesque image, their poor frail bodies thrashing about, as if some invisible force was beating them senseless. A putrid black oil poured from their mouths, and they continued to convulse, causing Ruby and Martha to scream in horror.

"Sisters! Stop the theatrics and say the words!"

screamed Lucinda. She tried to give Gothel an encouraging look, but Gothel could see she was just as frightened as Gothel was.

"Come on! Say it again, this time using all of our power!" screamed Lucinda.

Flower, gleam and glow
Let your power shine
Make the clock reverse
Bring back what once was mine

Heal what has been hurt
Change the fates' design
Save what has been lost
Bring back what once was mine . . .

What once was mine

Hazel and Primrose sputtered something unintelligible, spitting the black oil-like substance all over Gothel and the odd sisters. Their bodies seized one final time and then stopped so suddenly it startled the witches.

"Did it work? Did it work?" Ruby asked.

Gothel was slapping her sisters on the cheeks, trying to rouse them. "Hazel? Prim? Wake up! Hazel!"

Gothel was beside herself. She couldn't stop crying. She was slapping her sisters harder and harder, trying to wake them, until finally Ruby and Martha had to pull her off them. Lucinda put her face in front of Gothel's so she would have something else to focus on. "Gothel, look at me. Listen. They're gone. There is nothing we can do. We tried our best."

"No! I won't give up!" Gothel scrambled back to her sisters, clawing at the ground, trying to get to their bodies, as the odd sisters held her tight in their embrace. She made a terrible guttural scream that broke all the windows in the greenhouse, showering glass on all of them. Gothel was cutting herself on the glass as she struggled on the ground to get to her sisters. Lucinda put her hands over Gothel's eyes and said the word *sleep*, putting Gothel into a deep dreamless sleep, ending her pain. Lucinda couldn't stand to see Gothel in such torment. She couldn't imagine what Gothel must be feeling. Losing her sisters was Lucinda's greatest fear.

Her heart broke for Gothel, and for Primrose and Hazel.

At least Primrose and Hazel have each other in death, she thought.

Gothel was now alone.

CHAPTER XVIII

SISTERHOOD LOST

Gothel slept as if in a fairy tale. Almost endlessly. Her sleep was not a curse; it was a blessing bestowed by the odd sisters, who had been sent away by Jacob in the chaos after Hazel's and Primrose's deaths. Lucinda, Ruby, and Martha left without a fuss but not before leaving Gothel with one more enchantment. One more bit of magic.

"We are so sorry for your loss, little witch," they said to her as she slept.

"The world is dark, selfish, and cruel. If it finds the slightest ray of sunshine, it destroys it," said Lucinda. "Do not wake until your heart heals," she whispered in Gothel's ear, kissing her on the cheek before she took her own sisters by the hands to make their way out of the dead woods.

Jacob thanked the sisters and promised to care for his queen. "Call on us if you need anything at all, Jacob," Lucinda said as they reached the thicket. He promised he would but didn't intend to keep his promise. "We've left a raven, Jacob. Please send it if Gothel needs anything."

Jacob nodded as he watched the sisters pass through the thicket like wraiths. The sight sent a chill through him he hadn't known was possible. He was relieved to see the sister witches go. But he quickly turned his mind to his little sleeping witch.

He had never in all his years been without a queen in the dead wood. His little witch hadn't taken the blood, and even if she had, she couldn't rule while she slept. He had no choice but to act as regent.

He arranged majestic crypts for Hazel and Primrose, with stunningly beautiful weeping angels in the image of Gothel, just to the left of the courtyard. Their crypts and weeping angels flanked the tree-lined path that led to the city of the dead, right on the border of where their legions of minions slumbered. . . . He had almost entombed them in their own corner of the city, but he knew the soil there was still steeped in Manea's magic. He had vivid waking nightmares of Hazel and Primrose rising from the dead to do his bidding. The thought terrified him. He was seized with worry that Gothel would try to resurrect her sisters in that fashion in a fit of grief when she woke. So he instructed his minions to place the crypts carefully on the border and to remove from Gothel's library all of Manea's books that pertained to necromancy, for fear she would foolishly try something out of desperation.

He would tell Gothel the books had been destroyed. He would lie. It wouldn't be the first time. Gothel hadn't read the entry about him in her mother's book closely enough. She had misunderstood the meaning. Yes, he was bound to her, but not in the way she supposed. His duty was indeed to protect her. So he would hide the books. He would keep her from making foolish choices. He would protect her. He would lie.

Jacob wondered if Gothel would ever wake. As the years passed, he contemplated writing the triplets. So many years passed, more than he could count, and Gothel just slept with Jacob at her bedside under the glass dome of the morning room so the potted rapunzel flower on her bedside table would receive enough light. He often said the words written by Manea that Gothel had recited in the greenhouse so the flower would keep Gothel young. Thus, time did not diminish Gothel's young face or raven hair as she slept, even though the landscape around her changed by the year. She remained forever timeless with the help of the flower and perhaps with the triplets' enchantment as well. Jacob didn't know.

Finally, he decided to write the sisters. Their raven had been waiting and watching in one of the largest trees in the dead woods. It had made a home for itself, the only living creature in the woods aside from Gothel. It sometimes circled around the woods, screeching, but it always returned to its tree. Jacob made sure his minions left food for the raven every day, in a wooden bucket at the base of the tree. And he sometimes saw the raven drinking from or bathing in the Gorgon fountain. He didn't question how the raven lived so long. Jacob had served many witches over the years and had seen stranger things. His experience told him that if the raven was still alive, the triplets were likely alive as well. So he sent a simple letter with the raven, asking the triplets for help. Asking them to wake his grieving little witch. The dead woods had gone without a queen for far too long. The world around it was changing, and he was starting to become fearful for his little witch's well-being.

But the witches never came; instead they sent Jacob the incantation to wake Gothel himself. They lamented their inability to come themselves. They sent their many apologies—written in three different hands—all of them sincere, and all of them full of worry about Gothel. They promised they would come when they could, but they weren't sure when.

Their own little sister, Circe, was in peril, and they were doing everything they could to save her. They promised if they hadn't been terribly occupied with their own ordeal, they would have come to see Gothel through her grief themselves.

They would come when they could. If they could.

In their place, they sent their cat, Pflanze. She was a beautiful feline with tortoiseshell markings, black, orange, and white. Her eyes were large and bewitching, and she seemed always to be taking one's measure. Her paws were white, like fluffy marshmallows, and she was often adjusting them, shifting her weight from one to the other, almost like a little dance, all the while looking straight into Jacob's eyes, as if daring him to ask her what she was thinking. When she arrived in the dead woods shortly after the raven came back, Jacob knew she was no ordinary cat. Magical creatures always knew each other on sight, or perhaps it was smell. Jacob wasn't sure which. He was sure, however, that the cat was there to help. And he knew from the start that he liked her, though he could tell she didn't think much of him.

Jacob put off performing the incantation the odd sisters had sent. He dreaded Gothel's grief. He feared what she might do. He didn't want to break her heart all over again. He didn't want to see the realization that she had lost her sisters wash over her again. But the dead woods needed its queen. And perhaps in her grief Gothel could be a proper queen of the dead, having experienced the greatest loss one could imagine.

The loss of sisterhood.

Pflanze hopped onto Gothel's bed and snuggled beside her as she slept, as if comforting her before she woke. *It's time, Sir Jacob. It's time to wake your queen.*

Jacob heard the cat's voice in his head the way he used to hear Manea's when she didn't use her actual voice—clearly, as if she were speaking aloud. He didn't question the cat's ability to communicate that way. The cat had been sent by three powerful witches—witches so powerful even Manea feared them. Jacob had never shared Gothel's notion that she was one of the witches from her mother's vision. He knew it was Lucinda, Ruby, and Martha. But he did start to doubt Manea's interpretation of the vision. He wondered if Manea hadn't brought all of this about herself. *Never mind,* he told himself. *Never mind.*

Pflanze's voice filled his head. *There is a reason many of our ancient stories involve self-fulfilling prophecies, bringing doom to the visionary.*

Jacob didn't respond. He knew the cat was right. He took the letter the triplets had written out of his jacket pocket and read the incantation to his sleeping queen.

Wake the grieving sister
Bring her to the light
Send all thoughts of grief away
And chase away the night

Gothel's eyes opened slowly, adjusting to the light coming in from the domed ceiling. She looked around the room as if searching for something—or someone. She sat up and started to cry silently.

"They're dead, aren't they? It wasn't a dream?" she said, tears running down her face.

"No, my little witch, it wasn't a dream. I'm so sorry," said Jacob as Gothel fell back to the bed with tears still in her eyes.

"Then Mother was right. I guess I am destined to be alone after all."

❖ ❖ ❖ ❖

Gothel woke up in the carriage house. She didn't know how she had gotten there. The last thing she remembered was being dragged out of Hazel's crypt, but the memory was hazy in her mind. She did remember seeing the words written on her sisters' crypts as she was being pulled away.

Sisters. Together. Forever.

Jacob had had the words carved into the stone. He had done it out of respect. He hadn't known it would rip at Gothel's heart to see it there, a reminder that she had failed her sisters. She wanted to be with them, even now. But then Jacob would just drag her out again, wouldn't he? She didn't even remember going to see her sisters' resting place. She remembered waking up in the morning room, and then waking up here in the carriage house. She didn't even know how long she had slept, how long her sisters had been in their graves.

And Jacob couldn't tell her. "Time means nothing in the dead woods," he had said when she asked him earlier.

It could have been days or it could have been hundreds of years. Gothel didn't know. She could see through the carriage house window that there were spires beyond the thicket, a castle. No longer was she surrounded by small villages filled with simpletons. There seemed to be a number of more sophisticated hamlets on the edge of a bustling city, and in the distance a flourishing kingdom. All right outside her thicket. How many years did it take to build a kingdom? *Surely Jacob saw this happening around him while I slept,* she thought. Maybe the odd sisters knew how long she had slept. *I should ask them,* she thought. Did the sister witches track the time where they lived? She would have to ask them if they ever made their way to her again.

In the meantime she had their cat—a cat who just stared at her, watching her every move.

Even though much had changed outside the thicket, within the boundaries things were much the same. The years had not diminished her sisters; she had seen them when she went into their crypts, before Jacob pulled her out and brought her to the carriage house to rest. She was thankful death had not taken her sisters entirely. They looked as they always had. Sleeping, and beautiful. Her sisters. Together. Forever. Jacob had placed their mausoleums right on the border of the enchanted soil, close enough to preserve them but not close enough to raise them from the dead.

Jacob is clever, she thought. He and the odd sisters had seen to everything. They had even seen to her grief and provided her a companion in Pflanze. She felt robbed. Robbed of her memories, robbed of her sisters, and robbed of her grief. She didn't even know how long she had been awake.

It was yesterday. You woke yesterday. You insisted on seeing your sisters. We told you you weren't strong enough yet, but you insisted, and you fainted from exhaustion. Jacob put you here. It was closer than the main house.

Gothel looked around sharply. Was she hearing things now, too?

My witches did not rob you of your grief, young witch. They gave you the peace of mind you need to focus on bringing your sisters back. Isn't that what you want?

It was Pflanze. She was sitting on the edge of the bed, looking at Gothel with her dazzling eyes. Gothel laughed. She had thought there was more to that cat than she was letting on. Leave it to Lucinda and her sisters to send her a talking cat.

"Of course that is what I want! But how do you suppose I do it?" Gothel asked.

I haven't a clue. But you seem to think it has something to do with a flower.

"The flower! Yes. But one rapunzel flower isn't strong enough to bring back the dead."

It's clearly strong enough to keep you young all these years while you slept.

"Oh! How long did I sleep? Maybe there's more rapunzel!"

Gothel got up to go to the greenhouse, but she fell right back onto the divan. She felt faint and weak and couldn't stand without getting dizzy.

You have to rest, Gothel. You were under an enchantment for a long time. Apparently, it's exhausting to sleep for so many years.

"Apparently." Gothel sighed. "Would you mind finding Jacob for me? I need to speak with him."

He's right outside the door. He is never very far away from you if he can help it. He's been very worried about you, young lady. Please give the poor creature some peace of mind and let yourself heal.

There was a knock on the door. It opened before she could tell the person to come in. It was Jacob. "Gothel!"

"Jacob, I'm so sorry. I promise I won't try to get up again until I'm healed. I'm so sorry I worried you."

"No, Gothel, listen. I have a carriage and some

wagons ready to take you and Pflanze out of here. I've already sent a raven to Pflanze's mistresses to let them know where they can find you. You need to get out of here at once!"

"What do you mean? Why are you sending me away?"

"The kingdom is marching on the dead woods as we speak. They will be here within the hour, and I need you well away before they arrive."

"Why? Why are they coming?"

"They want the rapunzel, Gothel. Their queen is ill and needs it. She is expecting a child, and the King is willing to do anything to save his queen and their baby."

"But how do they know? I don't understand. Who could have told them about the flower?"

"I don't know, Gothel. I'm so sorry."

"I can't leave without my sisters! Without the flowers."

"I know. I've put your sisters in wooden crates filled with all the rapunzel flowers. The flowers should keep them preserved during your journey.

I made provisions should something like this ever happen. I have arranged a cottage for you and your sisters far from here."

"You ripped out all the rapunzel?" Gothel was horrified.

"I had no choice! There is no time, Gothel! You have to leave at once!"

"How long will it take to get to this cottage? How far away is it? Will the flowers last?"

"They should last the journey," he said.

"What am I supposed to do with dead flowers?"

"There are more at the cottage. I sent out my man to plant them for you many years ago while you slept." Jacob was getting impatient.

"How do you know this cottage is really there? How do you know it wasn't this man who told the King about my flowers!"

"I trust this man, Gothel. Now I need you to trust me. The cut flowers' power should last long enough to get you to the cottage. And I hope you will have enough flowers growing at the cottage to revive your sisters."

"But what about you? Won't you come with me?"

"I have to stay here and defend our lands. We need to make them think we are fighting to keep the one flower we have here."

"I can't leave you alone, Jacob. How will I know what happens to you? How will I know you are okay?"

"I will write you once it is over. If you've not heard from me in a fortnight, then you know it didn't go well for us."

"Jacob, no! I won't leave you."

"Gothel! You have to go! You don't have your mother's powers. You cannot defend yourself against this army. I cannot allow you to stay here and be slaughtered. It is my duty to protect you! The wagons are laden with trunks filled with your mother's books, your clothing, everything you will need, and as many chests of your gold as the wagons can carry. Now please, leave at once. I do not wish to bundle you up like a disobedient child, but I will if I have to."

Gothel saw the desperation on his face. She saw she hadn't a choice. She looked at her friend—for that was what he was—and smiled. She knew she would never see him again, and he was giving up his afterlife to save her, and her sisters.

"Okay, Jacob, help me to the carriage." She picked up Pflanze and slowly walked through the courtyard while holding Jacob's arm with her free hand to steady herself. She knew she would never see the dead woods again. And she knew her mother had been right: she had destroyed the dead woods. She was the witch from her mother's vision. Not the odd sisters. She was the reason everything would turn to dust. This would never be happening if her mother were still alive. Then she remembered.

"Jacob! The blood! Is it in one of the crates?"

"Yes, my little witch. I hope one day you decide to take the blood and you come back to reclaim the dead woods."

"I will, Jacob! I promise. And on the day I return, I will bring you back."

"Please don't, my lady. As much as I love you,

I think I would at last like some peace. To rest."

"Of course, Jacob. You deserve that," she said, kissing him on the cheek.

"Thank you, my little witch. Now go. Don't look back. I couldn't bear to see you looking back at me while you go," he said as he helped her and Pflanze into the carriage.

"I won't, Jacob. But know that I will miss you terribly. And know that I love you."

"I know, little one. I know." He gave her one small good-bye kiss on the cheek and slammed his skeletal hand on the side of the wagon to let the driver know it was time to depart.

It wouldn't be until many years later that she would wonder how the soldiers had been able to break through the protective enchantment of the forest. For now, Gothel's heart raced along with the horses as they sped down the dirt road taking Gothel to her new home.

Leaving the world she knew behind.

CHAPTER XIX

GOTHEL'S NEW HOME

"I thought they would be here before now," said Ruby, squinting as she looked down the road, hoping to spy Gothel and Pflanze's caravan making its way.

"We would have seen them if they were on the road, Ruby," said Lucinda.

"Hope they're okay! We haven't heard anything since Jacob packed them off," Martha said, fretting and fidgeting with the lace on her dress.

The odd sisters looked around their friend's new home. It was a country house, really. Larger than a cottage, as Jacob had described it in his letter, but decidedly smaller than what Gothel was used to in the dead woods. The odd sisters thought Gothel could be happy there, though. There was a stone fence with a wooden gate at the road, and beyond were beautiful flowering cherry, almond, and magnolia trees, along with fragrant honeysuckle, jasmine, and lavender bushes. It was rather idyllic, the sort of house you read about in a romance story, with mossy stones, overgrown ivy, and trellises covered in roses. The sort of house a young woman and her sisters move to after their situations are reduced, but the reader is left confused, because it's a charming, beautiful house that anyone would be happy to have—so it's a wonder why the protagonists are moaning about the size of the sitting room, or lamenting over the parlor being too small to fit a piano.

The house was a two-story affair. Downstairs were the double parlor, kitchen, dining room, and a sitting room Gothel could use as her library. Upstairs were the bedrooms, one for each sister and a small one for a maid, should Gothel decide to take one on. And if Gothel chose, the large attic with exposed beams could be used to practice magic. The sisters thought Jacob had done well to find Gothel such a lovely home, surrounded by life and beauty.

The odd sisters had magically perched their own house nearby, just inside the boundaries of Gothel's new property in a lovely field of wildflowers, next to a creek with an arched bridge that took travelers to the closest town, where they could buy provisions and other sundries. On the other side of the field were rocky black cliffs overlooking the ocean. It really was a lovely spot.

"Perhaps they've stopped to rest in one of the neighboring towns?" said Ruby.

"I'm sure that's it," said Martha, clearly worried.

"Well, I think you two should stay here and wait for them while I go to town and get some things I know Gothel will need." Lucinda gave her sisters a smile and then added, "I won't be gone long," as she walked to their house, waiting in the wildflower field.

It was a charming green gingerbread-style house with a witch's cap roof, stained glass windows, and black shutters. When Lucinda got into the house, she waved to her sisters from the large round kitchen window and yelled, "Don't worry, Sisters. I'm sure they will be here soon! Perhaps even before I get back!" And off she went, her house rising into the clouds. It wasn't often Lucinda traveled in her house without her sisters. It was strange to see them so small down below with looks of worry on their faces. Perhaps it was strange for them, as well, seeing her leave without them. *Not to worry, my dears,* she thought. *I will be back with you soon.*

No sooner had she gotten into the clouds than it was time to land the witch's cap house in a lovely little town with rows of shops. There were dress shops, a butcher, an open-air market that sold all sorts of produce and herbs, and a baker who baked breads and made sweets in the shapes of animals. He had two large windows in the front of his bakery: one that featured his edible menagerie and one where he would show off his talents to the passersby likely curious about how he made his confections.

Lucinda loved the idea of Gothel's walking the cobblestone paths, awestruck by the shops. She almost felt guilty for doing the shopping for her, taking that pleasure away from her, but she knew Gothel would be exhausted when she arrived at her new home, and Lucinda wanted her to be comfortable in her new surroundings.

Lucinda's first stop was the dressmaker and notions shop. It was called Fripperies, which she found amusing. She noticed in the window of the shop there were little cards offering and requesting various services.

When Lucinda walked into the store, the brass bell overhead rang, getting the attention of the proprietress, who was busy behind the counter, putting away spools of ribbon. "Hello, may I help you with something?" asked the woman, eyeing Lucinda, who was suddenly thankful she had been thoughtful enough to wear something nondescript. She was wearing a simple dress the color of eggplants, trimmed in delicate black lace, and none of her normal ornamentation in her hair. She always found it was best to be as plain as possible when traveling in those small towns, and the last thing she wanted to do was draw unwanted attention to herself or Gothel.

"Hello, yes. Good afternoon," said Lucinda. "I noticed the advertisements in your window. I'm setting up a household for my dear sister, who will be arriving at her new home just one town over. I'm looking for a cook who is also willing to do the shopping, and perhaps a girl who can care for the house. May I fill out a card for your window?"

The woman behind the counter smiled at Lucinda, putting down her ribbon. She seemed to be considering something. "Well, I do have someone I think would be perfect for the position. She has good references. She's an older woman, mind you, but very hardworking. If it's a small home, she could probably manage everything."

Lucinda smiled at the woman. "As long as you don't think it would be too much for her. My sister would happily pay her more for the extra duties. When can you arrange to send her over?"

The woman handed Lucinda a number of hand-written references and a card with the woman's name printed on it. "Everything seems to be in order. I assume you've checked her references?"

"Oh yes."

Lucinda laughed. "I'm so sorry, I've completely neglected to introduce myself. My name is Lucinda White."

"A pleasure to meet you, my lady. And my name is Ms. Lovelace. This is my establishment. Has been for the past six years."

"A pleasure to meet you as well, Ms. Lovelace. I appreciate your help, and I admire your name. I assume I can count on you to contact this Mrs. Tiddlebottom and inform her we would be happy to have her fill our post?" asked Lucinda as she passed Ms. Lovelace a card with Gothel's address. And then she added, "And please do send along a young girl with good qualifications who can do the cleaning if Mrs. Tiddlebottom has any objections whatsoever with the amount of work that will be required."

Ms. Lovelace laughed. "Mrs. Tiddlebottom can always be counted upon to make her feelings known. I'll be sure to let her know that is an option. Don't you worry."

"Good, and we will provide a carriage to pick up her and her things when she is ready."

"I'll be sure to let her know. Is there anything else I can do for you?"

"Nothing at the moment, but I thank you," said Lucinda, handing Ms. Lovelace a small pouch of coins. "That is for your services, Ms. Lovelace. Thank you and have a lovely day."

"Thank you, my lady! Come again!"

The brass bell rang as Lucinda exited. She often laughed to herself when she saw the looks on people's faces when she told them her last name. Ms. Lovelace's only admission to knowing Lucinda was one of the King's relations was when she referred to her as "lady."

So, her cousin's name had traveled even to that great distance. *Never mind all that,* she told herself. *There is still much to do.*

She spent most of the afternoon wandering the various shops and placing orders to be delivered to

Gothel's new home. By the time Lucinda was done shopping, she had arranged the entire stocking of Gothel's larder and acquired bedding and various other things Gothel might need. Jacob had fortunately arranged the delivery of furniture when he'd bought the home some years ago, and he'd thoughtfully had it covered in white cloth to keep it from getting dusty until his little witch arrived. *Hopefully Ruby and Martha think to remove the cloths before Gothel arrives,* Lucinda thought.

Lucinda had only one basket to take with her on her trip back to Gothel's new home: the provisions for that evening's dinner. She wasn't sure how soon the deliveries would arrive and thought it best to take dinner home herself.

As Lucinda flew overhead, she could see Gothel's carriage and many wagons lined up outside her new home. *They must be inside,* she thought as she landed the house in the nearby field filled with beautiful yellow wildflowers. She saw her sisters run to the windows so they could see her land, excited to share the news that Gothel and Pflanze had finally arrived.

"Lucinda! Lucinda! They're here!" screeched Ruby and Martha.

Lucinda laughed. "Yes, I see that. How is our little witch?"

"Oh, she's exhausted!" said Martha.

"She's in torment!" said Ruby.

"All to be expected," said Lucinda. "And how's Pflanze?"

"Oh, she's thriving!" said Ruby.

"She's upstairs with Gothel now!" said Martha.

"Shall we stay and take care of our little witch, then, Sisters? She needs us now that she has no one else to care for her. At least until we can see her cook, Mrs. Tiddlebottom, settled in."

Ruby and Martha exchanged amused glances at the cook's name.

"Mrs. Tiddlebottom?" The three sisters laughed.

"Yes, her name is Mrs. Tiddlebottom. Contain yourselves."

"We won't stay too long, will we, Lucinda?" asked Ruby. "We still have the matter of Circe."

"Don't worry, Sisters. We won't stay long, I

promise. I just want to see that Gothel is in good hands. Shall we leave Pflanze here to keep an eye on things?"

Martha looked around to see if anyone was listening, as if Gothel would pop out from behind a curtain. "Do you think Gothel will share the flower with us, Lucinda? Have you seen it anywhere? I've searched everywhere."

"Shhh. I didn't sense it from overheard, either. Let's not bother Gothel with that right now. Let's go upstairs. I assume Gothel is resting?"

"She is! She's upstairs with Pflanze. Oh, Lucinda, she is in terrible shape. The long sleep has exhausted her," said Ruby.

"She lost her home, and her companion Jacob," said Lucinda.

"Not to mention her sisters," said Martha.

"We will do what we can to help her. We know all too well what it is like to lose a sister," said Lucinda.

"But we will get Circe back, won't we, Lucinda?"

"Yes, my dear, one way or another we will get her back."

Chapter XX

A World Without Her Sisters

"The flowers!" Gothel sat up in bed, panicked. "The flowers? Where are the flowers?"

Lucinda flew into the room. "We've found only one flower, Gothel. Only one. Likely the one Jacob had planted here years ago. It seems they did not flourish as Jacob hoped they might, but these are disenchanted lands."

"But what about my sisters? Where are they?" asked Gothel.

"Jacob thought to put enchanted soil from the city of the dead in their coffins, just enough to keep them preserved. But I'm sorry to say all the flowers that were placed with them in their coffins have died."

"How am I going to save my sisters?"

"I'm not sure, my little one. Our main concern has been your health."

Gothel was still befuddled from her long sleep. She was having a hard time clearing her head and a very hard time communicating. All she could manage was panicked rapid-fire questions as they popped into her head.

"The blood! Where is it? How long have we been here? Who did the unpacking?"

"We did, Gothel. We didn't want Mrs. Tiddlebottom to come across something that may frighten or confuse her."

"Who is Mrs. Tiddlebottom?"

"Your new cook, dear. She's completely trustworthy. We've made sure of that."

"Should I even ask?"

Lucinda laughed. "No, nothing like that. No magical interference, I promise."

"But what about the chests from the vault, where are they?"

"We put the gold in the cellar, along with your

sisters. You have the only key, Gothel. It's in your bedside table drawer. Mrs. Tiddlebottom has the keys to the rest of the house, of course."

"Where are my books?"

"In the sitting room. We've made it into a library for you. I promise we've arranged everything, while you've been sleeping."

"How long has it been?" asked Gothel, looking at the floral-patterned wallpaper. It was a pleasant deep brown and dusty rose. So different from her old home.

"Just a few days, Gothel. We've only been here a few days," said Lucinda.

"I feel like I'm living in an entirely different world," Gothel said, looking out the window at the sea of wildflowers and pink blossoming trees.

"You are, my dear, but it's a beautiful world, isn't it?"

"I suppose so," said Gothel. "Lucinda?"

"Yes, dear?"

"How long was I asleep in the dead woods?"

"A very long time, Gothel. More time than

I even realized had passed until I heard from Jacob."

"I need to go down to the cellar. I'm guessing Jacob packed my mother's blood with the other things from the vault," Gothel said, trying to get up but feeling faint.

"Let me. You're still rather weak. What should I look for?" Lucinda asked.

"A glass bottle of blood with a wax-sealed cork. It should be inside a wooden chest."

"I'll be right back! I'll send Mrs. Tiddlebottom up with some tea," said Lucinda as she fished the key out of the bedside table drawer.

Gothel had woken up in a world she didn't quite care for. It was a world without magic. Without Jacob.

A world without her sisters.

She had never imagined living in a world without them. She hardly knew what to do next. What was her life without the dead woods, without her sisters? Everything she knew had been destroyed or murdered. Even her beloved Jacob and his army were likely dust, her family home probably destroyed.

All so some ailing queen could have her precious flower.

Gothel was brought out of her musings by the sound of Mrs. Tiddlebottom's clearing her throat at the threshold of her room.

"Hello, my lady. Your sister asked that I bring up some tea."

"My sister?" asked Gothel. "Are my sisters here? Where are they?"

"Yes, my lady. Lady Lucinda has gone down to the cellar for something. The ladies Ruby and Martha are in the library," said Mrs. Tiddlebottom, giving Gothel a sad smile.

"Ah, yes, of course. Thank you."

"You poor dear. Your sister said you were still a little befogged after such a long illness. Now don't you worry, I will stuff you with your favorite foods, and hopefully liven your spirits!"

"Thank you, Mrs. Tiddlebottom," said Gothel, taking the tea.

"Now you drink that all up, Lady Gothel."

"Please just call me Gothel."

"And you can just call me Mrs. T," said Mrs. Tiddlebottom with a smile.

Lucinda walked back into the room empty-handed. "Thank you, Mrs. T. I think we will take our midday meal in the garden, if you don't mind. It's such a lovely day and I would like my sister to get some air."

"I think that's a wonderful idea, Lady Lucinda. I have some of her favorites in the oven now. I'd better go check on them before they're ruined," she said as she trotted out of the room and down the stairs to the kitchen.

"Did you find it?"

Lucinda shook her head. "I didn't, Gothel, I'm sorry."

"It has to be somewhere!"

"If it is here, we will find it, I promise!" Lucinda sat next to Gothel on the bed and put her hand on hers. "Listen to me. Your sisters are fine where they are now. They're safe. I know you're eager to wake them, and I understand, I do, believe me, but right now I'm worried about you. Can we focus on getting you better first? And once you're strong again, we can focus on your sisters. How does that sound?"

"Fine, I suppose."

"What's the matter?"

"Why did you tell the cook you're my sister?"

"This is a small town, Gothel. People gossip. You're a young woman with no family relations! I didn't want those nosy gossips in town weaving wild stories, digging up your background, or giving you any trouble. The last thing you need is the King sending his men to find the last remaining flower."

"That was very smart of you, thank you," said Gothel. "Have you heard from Jacob? Do you know what became of my lands?"

"I'm afraid there is nothing left of your lands—not much, anyway," said Lucinda with a sad look. She knew how much Gothel loved the dead woods.

"And Jacob?" asked Gothel.

"He's gone, too," said Lucinda. It seemed she had nothing but bad news for her friend that day.

"Then he is finally at rest," said Gothel, squeezing Lucinda's hand.

"Yes, he deserves his rest, don't you think?"
asked Lucinda.

"I do. I really do," said Gothel, wiping the tears
from her cheeks.

CHAPTER XXI

A LIFETIME ALONE

It had been several years since Lucinda, Ruby, and Martha had settled Gothel into her new home and then left her alone to flounder and blunder her way through her new provincial life, with the ever loyal and diligent Mrs. Tiddlebottom handling everything that might have otherwise occupied or distracted Gothel from her loneliness. They had even taken their cat, Pflanze, who, like her mistresses, was eager to see what would become of the odd sisters' little sister, Circe. To Gothel it was a lifetime.

Gothel had felt abandoned in those first months. The sisters and Pflanze had flown off in some invisible house to attend to matters far more important than Gothel, leaving her alone and defenseless with no magic.

Before the sisters left, Gothel's house had been thoroughly searched. Every single item that had been packed by Jacob was examined. Gothel and the odd sisters even pulled down every book to see if it had been hollowed out to hide Gothel's mother's blood. And after the sisters left, Gothel searched every item again just to be sure and because she had nothing else to do. She even emptied every chest of gold, not bothering to the put the coins back in their places. The blood simply wasn't there. It was gone.

Just like everything else in her life.

She felt her life had no meaning. No purpose. Even if she could wake her sisters, she wondered if that was what they would really want. And she wondered if they would be happy in that house, with its floral wallpaper and delicate furnishings. She remembered the day she had tried to bring her sisters back with the help of the odd sisters in the dead woods. The horrible scene flashed through her mind like a jolt.

Please let us die.

No, maybe it was best to let her sisters rest. Maybe it was time Gothel rested as well.

Gothel desperately wanted to see her sisters again, even if it meant being confronted by her mother. There was nothing for her here. Nothing but endless solitude, flower-patterned wallpaper, and something close to grief that she was not allowed to fully experience because the odd sisters had taken that from her also.

In her solitude, she began to dislike the odd sisters. They refused to come no matter how many ravens she sent, begging them to return. Her memory of them became distorted. Her loneliness started to twist her mind. The longer they were away, and the more letters they sent to say they couldn't come to see her, the more her love for them diminished. She started to distrust them, almost hate them. The odd sisters started to come in and go out of focus in her mind, changing from the girls she had known in the dead forest, the friends and sisters she had grown to love, to these creatures she'd invented. She couldn't tell them apart anymore. When the odd sisters did take time to write her, their letters were singularly obsessed with trying to save that sister of theirs. That Circe. And she wondered if it wasn't all just lies. They sent endless letters about her. Endless updates. Flowery, poetic letters, full of grief, worry, and love. Over the years, the tone of the letters started to change, becoming less coherent, and more disjointed. They said they'd finally devised a way to bring their sister back. A difficult spell they'd been working on for many years. They promised they would return as soon as they could. Gothel continued to plead for them to come to her. Even in her distrust of them, she had no one else but them—and, of course, Mrs. Tiddlebottom, who did her best to make Gothel happy. But no matter how Gothel pleaded with the odd sisters to return, there was always some reason they couldn't. First it was the matter of Circe, and then it was some nonsense about a dragon fairy-witch. It all sounded like twaddle to Gothel, like a fairy tale you told a child, and she started to wonder if Jacob had been right. She started to wonder if all this was their fault. And she wondered if her mother's vision had been correct. After all, her sisters hadn't become dreadfully ill until the odd sisters arrived for the solstice. It was as if they had appeared in the dead woods right out of the ether, under some pretense they were there to help, insisting they somehow knew Gothel needed them. Well, now it all sounded like rubbish. All of it. She needed the odd sisters, and they were nowhere to be found. Everything concerning them seemed suspect to her now. Now that she was old and ready to go into the mists. Now that there was nothing left for her in the world to love or care for.

She hadn't bothered using the flower. There were deep lines around her eyes, and her hair was starting to turn silver. It was a blessing Mrs. Tiddlebottom was farsighted. She often remarked that Gothel had become a soft blur, though she still managed to bustle around the kitchen and tend to her duties. But Gothel could see herself clearly in her bedroom mirror and had come to the conclusion that she had to have been asleep for a very long time in the dead woods. Long enough for the entire landscape to change. Long enough for the frightening tales of the queen of the dead to vanish and no longer inspire fear or respect. Long enough for Gothel to age considerably without the help of the flower. And she was thankful.

The older she was, the sooner she would die.

Soon I will be done with this world I despise and mistrust. Soon my light will vanish like my sisters'.

"Stop this nonsense!" said Lucinda, swooping into Gothel's garden like a wild harpy. "I won't have any such thoughts flooding your head!"

"What?" said Gothel, looking at Lucinda with surprise.

"No! We can't have our little witch contemplating such foolishness!" said Martha, joining her sister, hovering over Gothel.

"Yes, what would your sisters do if you left them?" said Ruby, also appearing out of nowhere.

Gothel stared at the odd sisters, wondering if

they were real. *They don't quite fit in this setting,* she thought. Then again, neither did she.

"Oh, I assure you we are real," said Lucinda, laughing. "We are very real indeed!"

"I can't believe you're actually here!" said Gothel, not trusting her senses.

"Why do you look so old? Where is the flower? Why haven't you been using it?" asked Lucinda.

"You haven't lost it, have you?" asked Ruby.

"No, it's still hidden among the yellow wild-flowers, out there somewhere." She motioned to the field of wildflowers.

"Are you sure?" asked Ruby, fretting and trying to spot it among all the other yellow flowers.

"Yes, of course I am. Why? Do you want to take that from me as well?"

"What are you talking about? We're here to help you, Gothel!" said Lucinda, clearly hurt by Gothel's words.

"You're here to help me? Really? After all this time? Now that I'm ready to die? I don't want to live in this world! I don't want to suffer in it alone. I can't have my sisters back, and I will never have my mother's magic! There's nothing to live for!"

"Gothel! Get up at once and come with us to the field! You will use the flower's magic to make yourself young again! And we will find a way to bring your sisters back! I promised we would help you, and we will! We have been fighting for our own sister's life!"

"I don't believe you!"

"Don't you? Would you believe me if I told you we put our lives at risk and scoured the ruins of your home in the dead woods to find your mother's blood?" asked Lucinda, her hand on her hip.

"You did?"

"Yes, Gothel. You know we love you. Look," said Lucinda, holding a small glass vial of blood in the palm of her hand.

"This isn't my mother's blood. This isn't the right bottle."

"The original was broken. Most of it was spilled on the floor of the vault. I salvaged what I could and brought it straight to you. You have been on our minds all these years, Gothel. I'm sorry time moved slowly for you in this place. I'm sorry you let yourself wither away, but time works differently for us. We don't know why. Now please, take this blood, Gothel. Be the witch you're meant to be!"

"Will it work?"

"There's only one way to find out."

CHAPTER XXII

WHICH WITCH IS WHICH?

Gothel woke up in an endless sea of yellow wild-flowers with the odd sisters looking down on her with their giant bulging bug eyes and goofy bird-like expressions. She hadn't noticed when they were talking earlier, but they somehow still managed to look young after all those years. Sure, they looked older than when they were girls together, but they looked so much younger than they actually were. She wondered if anyone would have guessed all of them were hundreds of years old.

"You're looking quite young again yourself," said Lucinda, reading Gothel's mind and offering her hand to help Gothel to her feet.

"Our time in the dead woods together as girls feels like a lifetime ago," said Martha.

"Many lifetimes, actually," said Ruby.

"It feels like yesterday to me," said Gothel.

"And yet since you've moved into this house, time seems to move slowly for you," said Lucinda.

"Come on, let's go into our house. It's closer. You passed out after you drank your mother's blood," said Martha.

"What house?" Gothel looked around, trying to find the house. The last time the odd sisters had visited, they spoke of the mysterious house, but she had been too exhausted to remark that she didn't know what they were talking about. This time it just seemed ridiculous, like everything else. Lost sisters. Dragon-fairy witches. Invisible houses. She was at her wit's end with the sisters.

"Calm yourself, Gothel! Really, now. Such uncharitable thoughts," said Ruby.

"Our house is right there," said Lucinda, pointing at it as if Gothel were clearly out of her mind.

"I don't see a house, Lucinda. You are always

talking about a house, but I've never seen it."

The odd sisters had worried looks on their faces. "What? What is it?"

"We're not sure," said Lucinda. "Come with us."

They took Gothel by the hand and led her to their house, which was only a few feet away.

From her pocket Lucinda took a pouch that contained a powder the color of sapphires. "Here, put your hand out." Lucinda poured a bit of powder onto Gothel's hand. "Now blow, in that direction."

When Gothel blew the powder into the air, the house started to materialize before her eyes. She couldn't help gasping at having the front door right before her nose. "Can anyone else see this house?"

The odd sisters laughed. "No, just us, and any other witches that may happen by. But I think Jacob chose this place for its lack of magical beings. I don't think we have to worry about any unwanted visitors knocking on our door."

Gothel seemed to be taking something in. "So I'm not magical, am I?" she said as they walked into the odd sisters' house. To the right was the living

room, with a large fireplace flanked by two enormous black onyx ravens, and to the left was a cozy
sunlit kitchen with a black-and-white checkered
floor and a large round window.

The odd sisters gave her a sad look. "You still
have the power of the rapunzel flower," said Lucinda.
They could see the endless wildflower field from the
window. "Jacob chose a good hiding place for it
here. I doubt anyone would find it even if they came
looking for it."

"Anyone can use the power of the rapunzel
flower! I'm not a witch! I'm not magical!"

"Maybe the blood just needs time to take effect,"
said Ruby.

"Yes, Gothel, try not to worry! You're a witch in
your heart!" said Martha.

"But I'm not! I'm not a witch! I'm not even
queen of my lands! I have no lands. I have no sisters!
I have nothing!"

"You have us!" said Lucinda. She turned to
Ruby and asked, "Will you make us some tea, dear?
Gothel is very upset."

"Yes! Of course!" said Ruby, rushing to the stove to put on the kettle and knocking a cake tin that was sitting on the counter onto the floor, making a terrible clamor. "Don't worry! The cake is fine!"

"Oh good! I was really looking forward to having some cake!" said Martha.

Gothel shot them the evil eye. "Never mind the cake!" she snapped.

"Well, it really is very good cake. It's our friend's special walnut cake. She baked it for us!" said Martha.

Lucinda gave her sisters a look. "Stop talking about the cake, you're driving Gothel mad with all this cake talk!" Then she took Gothel's hand in hers and said, "Don't you worry, Gothel! We consider you a sister. You know we do! It's not your fault you were denied your inheritance. It's not your fault your ancestors didn't pass down their powers and knowledge."

"Do you really think of me as a sister?" asked Gothel.

"We do!" said Martha, looking at her sisters for reassurance. "Don't we, Ruby?"

"Yes! Of course we do!" said Ruby as she was nervously fumbling for a cup for Gothel's tea.

"Do you think there is some kind of spell you could do? Something that would really make us sisters? Something that would let me share your powers?" asked Gothel. She could only imagine how she looked to the sisters. Sad and pathetic. Pleading. She hated herself for even asking them.

The sisters looked at each other nervously. "Oh, Gothel, I wish we could, but I'm afraid it's impossible," they all said together.

"I see!" she said, getting up from her seat and going to leave.

"No, really, Gothel! We just did a very powerful spell to bring our sister back! If we give too much of ourselves away, then we won't have—"

"Wait? Where did you get that spell?" asked Gothel.

"What do you mean?" asked Lucinda, trying to sound innocent, though thoroughly unconvincing.

"You know exactly what I mean! You got it from one of my mother's books, didn't you?"

"Yes, it's a variation of one of your mother's spells. I think you might find it very interesting, Gothel. If you would sit down and calm yourself, I will tell you about it. It concerns you, actually. I found it when we were looking for something to help your sisters when we were in the dead woods. Your mother—"

"I can't believe this! I may not be magical, but I'm not stupid! You didn't go to the dead woods to help me! You wanted my mother's magic!"

"Gothel, please calm down! I'm getting the tea! Every conversation is better over tea!" said Ruby, still fumbling in the cupboards for the teacups.

"And cake, don't forget the cake!" called Martha.

"Yes, cake! Let's slice the cake," said Ruby, clapping her hands, clearly very excited about the cake.

"Sisters, please! Stop with the cake!" said Lucinda. Then, patting Gothel's hand, she said, "Gothel, listen to me. We told you we wanted access to your mother's books. We never kept that from you. What is this all about?"

"Did you even give me my mother's blood?"

Gothel's entire face changed. She seemed more like a woman who should be the queen of the dead than the odd sisters had ever expected. A queen without her lands.

"What?" asked Lucinda, taking her hand off Gothel's like it hurt her to touch it.

"You heard me! Was that actually my mother's blood you gave me? Jacob warned me you would destroy the dead woods! He told me you would take everything from me!"

"Of course that was your mother's blood!" said Ruby, becoming hurt and angry.

But Gothel wasn't listening. "What really happened to the rest of my mother's blood? Did you take it? What am I thinking? Of course you did! How else would you have the power to bring your sister back?"

"Gothel, that is enough! After everything we have done for you! This is how you treat us?" said Lucinda.

Ruby rushed over to Gothel, her hands trembling. "Gothel, here, take this." Ruby handed her a cup of tea. "You really need to calm down. You're starting to upset Lucinda! And look at Martha, she's ripping her dress!"

"I'm not ripping my dress! You were just ripping yours!" said Martha, her eyes wild.

Gothel saw there was dirt caked under Ruby's nails when she handed Gothel her tea. "Ruby! What's that?" She tried to snatch Ruby's hand, but Ruby pulled it away too quickly.

"What's what?" asked Ruby, quickly putting her hands inside the pockets of her skirt.

"On your hands! What's that on your hands?" Gothel demanded.

"Oh! I don't know." She shoved her hands deeper into her pockets. "What's wrong with you, Gothel? You're acting deranged!" Ruby said, backing away from Gothel. "I think it's time we cut the cake!"

"Take your hands out of your pockets right now! I want to see them!" said Gothel, raising her voice and advancing on Ruby, causing her to back away again and knock into the kitchen counter.

"No!" screamed Ruby. "I won't! Stay away from

me, Gothel!" Ruby started to panic. "Lucinda, Lucinda, calm her down! Get her away from me!" Ruby ran to the big round window and covered her ears. "Get her away from me! Get her away from me!" She said it again and again, but Gothel didn't let Ruby's fit distract her.

"Let me see your hands!" Gothel insisted.

Ruby nervously looked from Gothel to Lucinda to Martha. "Gothel, calm down right now or Lucinda will put you to sleep, I'm warning you!"

"Show me your hands!" screamed Gothel. Her face was contorted with rage, frightening Martha, who was laughing nervously and trying her best to make light of the situation. Lucinda just stared at Gothel with a mixture of horror, resentment, and heartbreak on her face.

"Stop it, Gothel! You're ruining everything! How are we supposed to have cake and tea with you acting so hysterical?" asked Martha.

Lucinda smiled. "Go ahead, Ruby, show her," she said in a very serious matter-of-fact tone, causing all the women in the room to stop their theatrics and turn their attention to her. "Don't be nervous, dear. Gothel can't hurt you," she said reassuringly. "After all, Gothel isn't even a witch."

Ruby and Martha gasped—and Gothel looked as if she had been smacked in the face. She was hurt by hearing Lucinda say that aloud. She had known it was true. She had known it in her heart, but to hear Lucinda say it like that, with so much malice, made it seem real for the first time.

Gothel stood there, just looking at them. Really looking at them for the first time since they had come back. Sometimes we create images of the people we love and hate in our minds, and those images override what we see with our eyes, even when they are right in front of us. Even if we've imagined them to be monsters, to see them as they truly are with our eyes and our hearts is sometimes shocking. Gothel was seeing the odd sisters differently, more clearly. She was seeing them for who they were on that day, not as the young girls she carried in her memories. Or the villains she had made them to be while they were away. She was seeing who they were in that moment, and she found they were much changed. Even though they were not old and withered, time had marred them in other ways. Time had changed their spirit. There was something sinister about them. Something wicked she hadn't seen in them when they were younger. And if she had seen that wickedness back then, it had been only a spark. A potential for evil, but not evil itself. Now that evil was blazing like a fire within them.

It was almost as if they weren't the sisters she had known when they were all young together. And they weren't entirely. Something was wrong. Something was different, perhaps missing. She couldn't quite place it.

"Gothel, please stop this nonsense!" said Lucinda.

"Oh please! I know why you're here! For the flower! Now tell me the truth, did you take it?" asked Gothel.

"Yes! We took it!" screamed Martha. "We're sorry! We had to! It's not what you think, Gothel! It really isn't!"

"We made sure you used it before we took it,

though, didn't we, Gothel? Now calm down and I'll bring you some cake!" said Ruby, ripping at the lace on her dress and scattering it on the black-and-white checkered kitchen tiles.

"How could you do this to me? All of this has been lies from the start, hasn't it? You never cared about me or my sisters!" Gothel's face was full of rage; she was like a wild beast ready to rip out the odd sisters' throats.

"No! If you would just listen to us, you'd understand! We shared with a friend the spell we used to get Circe back. She is like a daughter to us, and something went horribly wrong. She isn't the fairy-witch she used to be, and it's our fault! We need the flower to help her heal!" said Martha, backing away from Gothel in fear.

"More lies!" screamed Gothel.

"No! We love you! We do! We were going to just borrow the flower to try to help Maleficent, and then we were going to bring it back. I promise!" said Ruby, reaching into a nearby cabinet. "Look! We put it in a special pot so it wouldn't wither. And we enchanted the soil. We won't hurt the flower, we promise!" Ruby showed Gothel the flower. "Look! We took every precaution. We know how much the flower means to you. We would never do anything to hurt it or you!"

"Why didn't you just ask me for the flower? Why try to steal it?" asked Gothel.

Ruby and Martha were pacing around the room, fretting and ripping at their dresses and tearing the feathers out of their hair. "We don't know! We don't know! Oh, Gothel, we are so sorry!"

"Sisters, be quiet!" yelled Lucinda. "Look at you! You look dreadful! Stop that at once! I won't have you begging this sorry excuse for a witch for forgiveness!"

"Why do you really need the flower? Please tell me!" said Gothel, crying.

"Please, Gothel, stop your crying at once! We're telling you the truth. We need it for our friend," said Lucinda, who looked extremely vexed at being surrounded by hysterical women.

"But what about me? I'm your friend! You say I'm

like a sister, yet my actual sisters have been dead for hundreds of years and you've done nothing to help me bring them back! They're lying in the cellar with what's left of my family's legacy as I molder away in this prison of a house! I feel like Jacob must have felt while waiting for my mother to summon him. That's what I do, wait for you to come and swoop in and tell me everything will be okay, and it never is!"

"Gothel, you could have pored over your mother's books and found a way to wield her magic! All the answers are in those books you have stashed away in your library. If you really wanted to save your sisters, you would have found a way! You could have learned the spells, and you could have found a witch to teach you. But you never did. It's your fault, not ours!" said Lucinda.

"You were supposed to be those witches! You don't think I've heard the stories about you? Things you did while I slept! You think you can hide who you've become from me? It wasn't hard to put all the gossip together! Triplet witches. Terrorizing little girls! Your treachery is legendary! And now you're telling me you've made a mistake with the Dragon Witch? The Dragon Witch who destroyed the entire Fairylands? Who are you really?"

Lucinda's rage was starting to mount. "We are your sisters! We love you! Now stop this nonsense!" But Gothel was still in hysterics. She wanted answers. She was determined to find that the odd sisters had betrayed her in some way.

"Tell me how Circe died! Tell me what happened to her! In one letter, you say she was lost. In another she died. Now you say you have her back! Tell me the truth!" Gothel's face was splotchy and red, and her eyes were swollen from crying.

"Gothel, I will tell you, but you have to calm down and really listen to me. She was killed when Maleficent destroyed the Fairylands." It looked as if it hurt Lucinda to say it aloud, like the words ripped at her heart.

Gothel's eyes widened. "The same Maleficent you're trying to help now? She killed your sister and you're trying to help her? By Hades you're either lying to me or you're more foolish than I thought!

257

Either way, you couldn't possibly care for me if you're willing to betray me for the witch that killed your sister."

"It wasn't her fault! She doesn't even know she did it! We've never told her. It would kill Maleficent if she knew!" screamed Ruby.

"We love her, Gothel! She was just a girl when it happened. She's like a daughter to us!" said Martha.

"What happened to the Dragon Witch? What went so terribly wrong?" asked Gothel, genuinely curious.

"She gave too much of herself away to create a daughter, and now she is left with nothing. Nothing but the worst parts of herself. And it's our fault! We didn't take things into account. We didn't factor that there were three of us to make Circe and only one of her to make Aurora. We're hoping the flower can heal her, make her whole again."

"And you shared this spell with her because you wanted to help, is that correct?" asked Gothel, becoming more hurt and disgusted with every answer she received.

"Yes, we did. But it went horribly wrong. She is more alone than ever," said Lucinda.

"You are vile witches who destroy everything you touch. You've used me, killed my sisters, destroyed my lands, and now you've ruined the Dragon Witch's life as well!" spat Gothel.

"We want to make it right. Please, let us use the flower," begged Ruby.

"No! I need it! I'm going to find a way to heal my sisters! You're right! I'm tired of sitting around waiting for you to help me. I need to help myself!"

"Yes! When we come back, we will help you find a way to save your sisters. We promise, just as soon as we've helped Maleficent!"

"Fine, bring me with you! It's my flower and if you're going to use it, I want to be there to make sure it's protected."

The sisters looked at each other, stupefied. "That's not possible. You don't have any powers. It would be dangerous for you," said Lucinda, clearly tired of the conversation.

"Then do the spell that makes me your real

sister, and we will use the flower to heal the Dragon Witch. And then we will heal my sisters together." Gothel was desperate. She knew the odd sisters were powerful witches and there really wasn't anything she could do to keep them from taking the flower.

"If you knew how magic worked, Gothel, you'd understand we can't do that. Not all at once, at any rate. There must be time between powerful spells."

Gothel looked down at the floor. She saw little bits of red cloth from Ruby's skirt scattered on the tiles, and she thought of blood. And then she remembered: she had no choice. She couldn't let the witches take the flower from her. It was her only source of magic, her only chance to save her sisters. She said the words and wished with all her being they would help and guide her.

"Then I call upon the old gods and the new. Bring life to the dead, and give me my due!"

"What are you doing, Gothel?" said Martha, worried by hearing her say an incantation.

But Lucinda laughed. "Oh, look, Sisters. Gothel thinks she's doing a spell!"

Martha and Ruby joined in Lucinda's laughter, and it grew so loud the teacups started to rattle on their shelf, and the cake tin was vibrating on the counter, threatening to fall on the floor again.

"I call upon the old gods and the new. Bring life to the dead, and give me my due!"

"Gothel, this is just silly! Stop embarrassing yourself!" said Lucinda.

The odd sisters' house started to shake so violently it knocked their teacups and knickknacks off the shelves.

"Sisters! Stop your laughing!" But Lucinda realized it wasn't their laughing that was causing their house to shake. It was Gothel's spell. The house was shaking so powerfully the windows were bursting out of their frames and the odd sisters had to hold on to each other to keep from falling.

"Gothel! What are you doing? Stop this!"

"I call upon the old gods and the new. Bring life to the dead, and give me my due!"

Gothel screamed the incantation, her face transforming into something sinister. The odd sisters had never seen her like that before. She looked like an entirely different person. Focused. Confident. Queen of the dead. And utterly terrifying. It was as if she was channeling her mother.

Gothel flicked her hand, causing the flowerpot to fly out of Ruby's hand and into hers with such a powerful force the pot cracked in it on impact.

"Gothel!"

"I call upon the old gods and the new. Bring life to the dead, and give me my due."

Gothel pushed the hair away from her face the way her mother always had when she was about to do powerful magic. She gathered all her hate and pain and felt it surging through her body. She could actually feel it; it was like a white-hot ball in her stomach that was growing so large she could no longer contain it. She felt her hands shake and realized the rage would consume her if she didn't release it. She reached out her hands, which looked familiar and yet other to her—they looked like her mother's—and she released a torrent of lightning into the floor, causing the house to shake more violently than before.

"Gothel, stop! You're going to kill all of us!"

The witches could see the earth outside exploding violently, bringing forth a legion of skeletal creatures that swarmed the odd sisters' house, clambering to get through the doors and windows. The sound of their bone fingers scratching on the windows and wood was terrifying. Their awkward and broken bodies were pouring through every broken window like a plague.

"Gothel, no! Tell them to stop!"

"You will never have the flower!" screamed Gothel. "Never!" She stretched out her hand, grasping at the air, tightening her grip on something invisible, causing the odd sisters to fall to their knees and scream in pain as she brought her hand down in a quick motion. "Keep still, witches!"

"Gothel, please stop this! We don't want to hurt you!"

Gothel laughed. "Look at poor powerless Gothel now! What was it you called me? Silly?"

Lucinda's face was filled with pain. She struggled against Gothel's spell and slowly got to her feet. "Gothel! Stop this at once!" She slammed Gothel with a powerful blast, causing Gothel to fly backward through the large kitchen window and smash against the apple tree in the witches' garden. The blast scattered the skeletons in every direction, rendering most of them to dust.

Gothel found herself lying in the wildflowers, littered with the remains of her minions. She was covered in bruises and had deep gashes on her arms from going through the odd sisters' kitchen window. She thought her face might be bleeding as well. She wasn't sure. She just lay there, staring at the odd sisters' house as it rose into the sky. She sat up, clutching the flowerpot in one hand and flinging her other hand at the odd sisters, trying to direct lightning at them, but nothing came forth. There was no lightning. There was no magic. She watched them, with their bug-eyed expressions of astonishment, disappearing into the clouds. And from her life.

CHAPTER XXIII

MRS. TIDDLEBOTTOM'S SITUATION

"Gothel! Gothel! What in heavens happened?" It was Mrs. Tiddlebottom. She was tottering into the field, kicking broken bones and thick white ash as she rushed over to Gothel.

"I don't know, Mrs. Tiddlebottom."

"Here, take my arm, lady, let me see to those cuts." She examined Gothel's face. "I think I should call the doctor to come around the house. But I don't know if the message boy will be by this afternoon. Maybe I'd better go into town myself."

Gothel was heartened by Mrs. Tiddlebottom's concern. "I'm sure I will be fine under your

expert care, Mrs. T. Let's not bother the doctor."
Gothel could see Mrs. Tiddlebottom eyeing her; she
couldn't tell if Mrs. Tiddlebottom was looking at
the cuts or noticing that her face was younger now.
She wasn't even sure herself how young she looked.
She clutched the flowerpot as they went into the
kitchen, where she was instructed to sit down. "Put
that plant down, Gothel, and let me look at you!"
Mrs. Tiddlebottom went to a pantry to find her tinc-
tures and cotton strips. She soaked one of the cotton
strips in a deep reddish-brown liquid and held it in
her fingers, hesitating. "I'm sorry, lady, but this is
going to hurt."

⚜ ⚜ ⚜ ⚜

Mrs. Tiddlebottom was by no means a gossip, but
her sister was. It wasn't long before the entire town
heard about the strange happenings at Lady Gothel's.
After the odd sisters left, Gothel had sequestered
herself in her library, and Mrs. Tiddlebottom was
at her wit's end trying to get Gothel to come out for
her meals, or for any reason at all. Mrs. Tiddlebottom
confided her concerns to her sister, who in turn told

the most notorious gossip in town. And before she knew it, Mrs. Tiddlebottom had a full-blown situation on her hands.

"Lady Gothel! Please come out. We have a situation." Gothel opened the door to her library. "What is it?" she asked. Her hair was wild, and her face was smudged with red and purple powder.

"Oh! Look at you, Lady Gothel, sorry to disturb you!"

"And look at you, Mrs. T. You're wearing spectacles!"

Mrs. Tiddlebottom blushed. "Yes, my sister got them for me. Speaking of my sister, lady, well, you see, she came by today." Mrs. Tiddlebottom was clearly distressed, and she was having trouble arriving at the point.

"Yes, you said there was a situation?" asked Gothel as patiently as she could. She wondered how she must look. Her hands were stained with magical powders, and she hadn't changed her clothes in more days than she could count.

"My lady, would you please come into the

kitchen with me? Conversations like this are always better over a cup of tea."

"So I have been told." Gothel laughed. She remembered the odd sisters saying something very much along those lines. "Of course, Mrs. T. Let's go into the kitchen."

In the kitchen Mrs. Tiddlebottom held out a chair for Gothel. "Here you go, my lady, sit." Gothel wished the old woman would just get on with it, but she reminded herself to be patient with her. She realized her cook was rather distressed.

"Here, Mrs. T. It looks as if you should sit down. You look peaked. I'll go get the tea." Gothel went to the cupboard and pulled out two teacups and the teapot that matched. It was a set from her home in the dead woods. "Hmmm . . . there's only five cups. What happened to the sixth?" she asked absentmindedly.

Mrs. Tiddlebottom looked up. "What's that, lady?"

Gothel realized she hadn't meant to say that aloud. "I'm sorry, I just noticed there were only five cups to this set. There used to be six. Never mind. I'm sorry, you had something important to tell me?"

Mrs. Tiddlebottom got up to see what set Gothel was talking about. "Oh yes, the Samhain set. The silver ones with the black skulls painted on them. Your sister Ruby said she broke one when she was having her tea in the garden."

Gothel wondered if that was true. She was, in fact, almost sure Ruby or one of Ruby's sisters had actually stolen the cup. *Come to think if it, there were quite a few little things from around the house that are missing.* "Never mind, Mrs. T. Sit down and tell me what the matter is."

"There's no other way than to say it straight out, lady," she said, clearly trying to be brave.

"Well, you know that is what I prefer. Please continue."

"Yes. Well, it seems the kingdom has sent soldiers here to find some flower they think once belonged to the queen of the dead."

"What? What will become of my sisters?"

Gothel was panicked. *How am I going to get my sisters' bodies out of here?*

"Your sisters, lady?"

"Never mind. We have to leave!" said Gothel, running into her library and grabbing her mother's most important books.

"Lady Gothel, stop! What is it?" called Mrs. Tiddlebottom, tottering after her. "What's the matter?"

"What is it? What is it? Mrs. T! Soldiers are coming here to destroy my home! They think I am the queen of the dead! They're going to burn this place down! I suggest you pack anything you have of value this moment!"

"Lady, calm down, please! Listen to me. I have an idea. Now, I don't want to know anything about what you have down in that cellar, or your library, or what you get up to with those sisters of yours, but I do know you're a good girl. You've always been very kind to me, and you don't deserve to lose your home. It seems to me all they want is that flower. If we give them the flower without a fuss, I think they will take it without much kerfuffle. We can plant it outside, pretend we never even knew it was there," said Mrs. Tiddlebottom with a resolve that surprised Gothel. "Better yet, why don't you steal yourself away down in that cellar when they come? I will pretend to be the lady of the house and let them find the flower without a fuss."

"No, Mrs. Tiddlebottom! I can't give them the flower!" Gothel snatched the flowerpot in her hands and squeezed it tightly. "I can't give it up! I can't!"

"I don't think we have a choice, lady." Mrs. Tiddlebottom put out her hand. "Now give it to me, and I will put it out in that field with the others."

"There has to be another way." But Gothel was worried the old woman was right. "I don't understand why they need it! They destroyed my home taking the last one! I thought the Queen was healed!"

"The queen is ill again. Her pregnancy caused her to relapse."

"But they have a flower! Why do they need another?"

"Well, she's eaten the other one, hasn't she?"

"Bloody fools!" Gothel was incensed.

She felt trapped. She couldn't just leave with the flower. The soldiers might find her sisters in the cellar. They might find them there anyway, even if Mrs. Tiddlebottom gave them the flower willingly. Gothel didn't know what to do. She wanted to run. She wanted to pack the old woman and her sisters on a wagon and leave, but she knew they would eventually find her. They would hunt her down as long as she had the flower in her possession, burning every home she ever made for herself. Maybe she should have let the odd sisters take the flower. At least then it would have been safe. Mrs. Tiddlebottom was right. There was no other choice.

"You're right, of course. We will let them find the flower," she said, pushing the flowerpot toward the old woman.

"You'd better get down to the cellar now, lady! Don't make a peep!"

"Now?" asked Gothel, looking out the window to see if she could see the soldiers coming. "Are they coming right now?"

"Yes, my lady. Please. Now go!"

"Are you sure you're going to be okay dealing with this on your own?" Gothel was squinting, trying to see down the road. "Do you have time to get the flower in the field before they arrive?"

"I do! Now don't you worry yourself over old Mrs. Tiddlebottom. I can handle any soldiers that come knocking on this door! Believe me! Now off with you!"

"Thank you, Mrs. T!"

"Get down there and don't come out until I come for you!" said Mrs. Tiddlebottom with a quick kiss on Gothel's cheek. "Down you go! Off with you!"

Gothel went into the cellar. She hadn't been down there since she'd first moved to the house, when she had frantically searched for her mother's blood. Gold coins were scattered all over the floor, and the chests were open, just as she had left them. And her sisters' coffins were there, just as they had been since they'd moved in. She hadn't seen her sisters' bodies since she left the dead woods. She was afraid to look at them, afraid they had started to decay. Afraid to see their faces.

Afraid they would wake up and accuse her of failing them.

She crept up on their coffins, like she was trying not to wake her sleeping sisters, and opened the lids. The sleeping beauties were side by side, still as lovely as ever. Still young, still fair, but dreadfully pale. It was as if all the color had been leached from their bodies. Even Primrose's beautiful red hair had turned white. They looked like ghosts made of opaque glass. Like fragile replicas of the sisters she loved. The oddest feeling came over her. It was as if her sisters were there but not there. She couldn't express it any better. To see them there but not feel them was the most disturbing thing she'd ever experienced. Her heart broke as if it was breaking for every loss she had ever had right there in that moment, and she thought she might die from the pain of it. She missed her sisters so much. She should have been trying to find a way to resurrect them all that time. It had been years since she woke up in the dead woods from her long slumber, and she chided herself for not having spent the time trying to find a way to bring them back. *And if those wretched odd sisters hadn't made me sleep for hundreds of years, I might have brought them back by now!*

So many years wasted.

"Oh, my poor sisters, I am so sorry. I promise I will find a way to bring you back."

She put her hands on her sisters' and something happened. Her hands started to glow, just a little, like the rapunzel flower, and the light was spreading into her sisters like cascading fireworks. The light started to grow within them, causing them to glow, just a little, making them look more alive, the color returning to their faces.

"Hazel! Primrose! Are you there?" They didn't answer. They were quiet and still. They were dead. But the power of the flower was doing something. Gothel looked down at her hands and saw that they were old and withered again, like bone covered in skin. Her sisters had taken all of the rapunzel's healing powers from her. She ran to the chests to see if one of her mother's mirrors was packed away, and found one she didn't recognize among some of her mother's other things.

She gasped. Her hair was entirely silver, and her face was withered and gray, like an old apple doll. She was so much older than she'd even realized. If she didn't get to the flower now, she would die.

She went to the cellar door to listen for voices. Maybe she could sneak out and get the flower before the soldiers came. But she heard Mrs. Tiddlebottom talking with someone in the kitchen.

"Oh, a glowing flower, you say? Well, I suppose you will find it out there with the other wildflowers. I sometimes see something glowing in the field out there, but I just thought it was fireflies. You're more than welcome to go out and look for it, kind sirs. By all means, if the King wants it, he is welcome to it! I'm just an old lady surrounded by beautiful flowers. What's one flower to me if the King wants it?"

The soldiers laughed. "You don't seem like a demon witch of the dead to us!"

Mrs. Tiddlebottom laughed with them. "My

goodness, no! Whatever gave you that idea?"

"We were told the queen of the dead took refuge here with the last of her flowers, but clearly that information isn't correct."

Mrs. Tiddlebottom laughed again. "Imagine me, queen of anything!" She was laughing heartily until she saw an old beggar woman creeping in the far end of the field near the sea cliff. "Oh!"

"What is it?" asked the King's soldiers.

"Oh, nothing, dears. It just occurred to me that you're likely hungry and thirsty after your long journey. Please sit down and have a slice of hazelnut cake and some tea."

"Oh, we can't, ma'am, but thank you," said a lanky soldier. He seemed to be all arms and legs, like a giant friendly scarecrow with straw yellow hair.

"Oh, I insist, good sir! The flower will still be there when you're done. I can't send you back to the castle with empty stomachs! What will the King think of poor old Mrs. Tiddlebottom if she sends his soldiers back with rumbling stomachs?" Mrs. Tiddlebottom took out the cake tin and opened it.

"Now just look at this cake and tell me you don't want a slice. It's chocolate hazelnut!"

"Maybe just one slice," the lanky soldier said, taking a seat at the kitchen table. "Can we manage some for my men as well?"

"Oh yes! And some tea! You can't have cake without tea! I'll put the kettle on! Now sit yourselves down right here while I make it!" She sat them with their backs to the window facing the field, where she saw a woman hovering over the glowing flower, its light becoming more pronounced as she spoke to it. Then the woman, old and haggard, saw Mrs. Tiddlebottom looking at her, so she quickly hid her face in the hood of her cloak and covered the flower with a basket.

"Now who is that?" muttered Mrs. Tiddlebottom, doubting it was Gothel as she had feared.

"Who is what, ma'am?" asked the guards, turning around to see what she was looking at. "Do you know who that is, ma'am?"

Mrs. Tiddlebottom shook her head as the soldiers ran out the kitchen door to the field. "It might be someone trying to take the flower!" she yelled, hoping if it was Gothel, she would hear her and hide herself away before the soldiers reached her.

Within moments Mrs. Tiddlebottom could see the light of the flower coming nearer and nearer as the soldiers made their way back to the house. "Ah, so this is what all the fuss is about?" asked Mrs. Tiddlebottom. "I never even knew I had it in my garden." The soldiers seemed to be eyeing her differently than they had before. "Now that you have your flower, would you still like that piece of cake?" she asked, pretending she hadn't noticed the change in their demeanor.

"Who was that in the field?" asked one of the soldiers. He was a hairy beast of a man, a bit like a great bear, with one long eyebrow.

"I wouldn't know, dear!" she said offhandedly. "Come back inside and have your tea."

"And you wouldn't be trying to distract us with cake and tea so someone could take the flower right out from under us, would you? Trying to hoard it for yourself?" he asked, giving her the eye.

"My goodness, no! I don't even know what the flower does or why the King would want it! I didn't even know I had it!"

"Is that so?" asked the hairy soldier, but before she could answer, they were distracted by a terrible crash.

"What was that?" asked the lanky blond soldier, looking toward the cellar.

Mrs. Tiddlebottom started to panic. "Oh, just rats! I have the cellar locked up until I can get the rat catcher here. They're terrible, those rats! I'm afraid to go down there!"

The soldiers were still giving her the eye. "Perhaps we'd better go down there and check," the lanky soldier said, but Mrs. Tiddlebottom changed the subject.

"So, this is the flower, is it? The source of all this fuss. So tell me, what does it do?"

The soldier clutched it a little tighter as Mrs. Tiddlebottom went near him. "It heals ailments, including old age," he said, looking at Mrs. Tiddlebottom's heavily lined face.

"Ah! I wish I'd known I had it, then! I might have used it on myself!" she said, laughing, and the soldier softened to her once again. "I don't know anything about magical flowers, but I do know a thing or two about regular ones, and I know they can die unless they're potted properly. Let me go get you something to transport the flower. I won't be more than a minute! We don't want it dying before you get it to the Queen."

"Thank you, ma'am," said the soldier, clearly feeling foolish for suspecting such a sweet elderly woman.

She returned with a flowerpot filled with soil. "Now let me take care of that!" she said as she snatched the flower out of the soldier's hands and proceeded to tuck the flower's roots gently into the soft soil.

"This will do fine!" she said, hoping they had forgotten about that noise they'd heard in the cellar.

"Now, who wants a piece of old Mrs. Tiddlebottom's famous chocolate hazelnut cake?"

CHAPTER XXIV

THE QUEEN OF NOTHING

The soldiers had taken their time eating cake and drinking their tea. It wasn't until sunrise that Mrs. Tiddlebottom saw them off with baskets bursting with ham and cheese sandwiches, a walnut cake, chocolate cookies, and other baked treats. "Thank you, Mrs. T!" called one of the soldiers as they started back to the kingdom.

"Good-bye, dears," she said, waving them away with a big smile on her face until she saw them disappear over the bridge. Gothel was waiting for her at the cellar door when she opened it.

"You poor dear! Come out of that cellar!"

"You were very impressive with those soldiers, Mrs. T! You really were! I think you've dispelled any notions that the queen of the dead lingers here."

"And does she?" asked the old woman. "Never mind," she said. "I don't want to know."

"I'm the queen of nothing," said Gothel, sitting on a chair and catching her breath.

"Was that you lurking out there in the field, my lady? I thought it was you, but . . ."

Gothel sighed. "I'm afraid that's another question you'd rather I not answer."

"Too right! Well then, what will you do now?" she asked, getting fresh teacups from the shelf and taking out the tea tin.

"I'm going to take the flower back! I'm going to the kingdom, I'm going to sneak in the castle, and I'm going to take the flower back."

"After all of this? After letting them take it, you're going to go right after them and take it back? I'm sorry, my lady, but are you batty?"

"We've come to a point where you're either going to hear the entire story or you agree to trust that I know what I'm doing and not ask me any questions. We can't have it both ways."

"Even if you do steal it, what makes you think they won't just come back here looking for it?"

"And bother the sweet little old lady who sent them home with half the larder? An old woman who didn't even know she had the flower to begin with? I don't think so!"

Mrs. Tiddlebottom seemed to be taking what Gothel was saying into consideration. "True. True," she said, filling the kettle with water and putting it on the stove. "I think you're right."

"Now listen, you don't have to stay if you don't wish. I wouldn't blame you, Mrs. T. What you did last night was very dangerous, and I appreciate it. I really do. So if you're uncomfortable with what I'm about to do, I completely understand. Just do me this one favor. Please stay here until I get back? You are free to go after I return if you're afraid the soldiers will put it together that it was me who took the flower."

"Has this to do with what you have hidden down in that cellar? Do I want to know what it is?"

"I will tell you if you really want me to."

"No, Gothel. I don't think I do."

CHAPTER XXV

THE BLOODY CHAMBER

It had been weeks since Gothel ventured to the kingdom, leaving Mrs. Tiddlebottom alone to manage the house and be the keeper of the keys. Gothel had given her the keys to the cellar and the library to add to her ring of household keys, but told her not to enter either room. Mrs. Tiddlebottom felt like the French fairy tale bride who was given the keys to the chateau and told she was welcome to enter any room she wished except one. Of course, the French bride did it anyway. But that is another story altogether.

Unlike the French bride, Mrs. Tiddlebottom didn't want to know what was in the cellar. The way she figured it, the less she knew, the better. Oh, she had her theories. And if she had allowed herself to sit down and think about it, she would have put it all together, and in reality, she had, but she chose to put it out of her mind. Over the years, Mrs. Tiddlebottom had become very good at avoiding trouble, and she wasn't about to go falling into a deep pit of it now. Because that was what she foresaw: trouble. Not that she was a witch and saw things in that way, but she had common sense and could see Gothel was about to bring trouble upon all their heads. *No need to make more trouble by going into that cellar. I don't need to know what's in there.*

Besides, she knew what happened to the bride in that French fairy tale when she entered the forbidden room. She lost her head when her husband came home, and ended up in the bloody chamber with his other headless brides. The memory of that story gave Mrs. Tiddlebottom the shivers. Thinking of those poor girls' bodies hung on rusty hooks in that room, their heads sitting under bell jars . . . *Put it out of your mind,* she told herself. She didn't think Gothel would do such a thing to her, but Mrs. Tiddlebottom had made it her business not to go around tempting fate. Or getting her head chopped off. Not if she could help it.

Fairy tales are written for a reason, she thought.

They were cautionary tales. And Mrs. Tiddlebottom might have been an old woman, but she wasn't stupid. She spent most of her days busying herself with the baking of pies and cakes. The kitchen was bursting with them, but she found that baking calmed her nerves, and she was, after all, very worried about Gothel. More weeks passed than she supposed might for Gothel to travel to the kingdom and back, and still there was no sign of Gothel. So Mrs. Tiddlebottom baked more pies and even more cakes and gave them to anyone who would take them.

And just when Mrs. Tiddlebottom started to worry something terrible had befallen her lady, Gothel arrived with a baby in her arms just like it was any other day.

"And who is this?" Mrs. Tiddlebottom asked,

looking at the beautiful little creature in Gothel's arms.

"This is my flower," said Gothel. "We should probably find someone to care for her until she is older." She handed the baby over to Mrs. Tiddlebottom like she was a sack of potatoes.

"Your flower looks an awful lot like a baby. . . ."

"A baby whose mother ate my flower."

"You mean this is the Princess? Gothel! What in fairy wings were you thinking of, taking this baby?"

"I didn't have a choice! What would you have me do? Her father's army destroyed my kingdom for something that didn't belong to them, and gave it to his queen, who bequeathed it to this creature! She is the only flower left! If my mother were alive, she would have destroyed them and their entire kingdom! They're lucky the only thing I took was their child!"

"I don't know about this, Gothel! What must they be feeling now? It's one thing to take your flower back, but to take their child . . . I just don't know!" said Mrs. Tiddlebottom.

"She *is* my flower! The only one left of its kind. They destroyed almost everything I had and took my only hope of ever seeing my sisters alive again! They're not the victims here, Mrs. T! I am!"

Gothel could see Mrs. Tiddlebottom wanted to ask her what she meant about her sisters but stopped herself. She seemed to be considering Gothel's words for some time while looking at the little wriggling creature in her arms. Finally, she spoke.

"And what should we call her?"

"Rapunzel," said Gothel, walking away from the old woman and the child and descending into the cellar without even looking back.

"Well then," said Mrs. Tiddlebottom to the baby. "What are we going to do with you? We can't very well hire some gossipy wet nurse, not when it's certain you've been spirited away from the royal family."

Gothel had become more reclusive since the odd sisters' last visit, and since "the situation," as Mrs. Tiddlebottom had called it. And she became even more so after she brought Rapunzel into their lives. She spent most of her time either down in the cellar or in her library. She would pop out once a day, take the baby into her arms, sing her a little song, and then rush back to whatever she was up to in the cellar.

With the help of her sister, Mrs. Tiddlebottom found a wet nurse for Rapunzel, one they paid handsomely to keep quiet about the baby. Mrs. Tiddlebottom had made up a story about one of Gothel's sisters having the child out of wedlock and said that was the reason for the secrecy. Mrs. Tiddlebottom thought it was the perfect ruse. She knew her sister wouldn't be able to keep the secret and would spread it far and wide. Gothel's sisters were often mentioned by wagging tongues in the village, and Mrs. Tiddlebottom made sure lady Gothel was made out to be some sort of saint for taking on her sister's burden. By all accounts, everyone in the village thought Gothel was like a fairy godmother to the child. Mrs. Tiddlebottom had made sure they paid Mrs. Pickle, the wet nurse, well, promising her the position of governess once the baby was older.

And Mrs. Pickle was a marvel, which was a miracle to Mrs. Tiddlebottom, who needed more help than ever around the house. Mrs. Tiddlebottom often thought Mrs. Pickle had been sent to her from the gods to help her raise the baby. And Mrs. Pickle was happy to have a child and a family to care for, and a place to call home. She took the small room upstairs and shared it with Rapunzel so she would never be too far away from the child. She watched her like a hawk and was ferociously protective of her. She never spoke of it, not even with Mrs. Tiddlebottom, but the old woman knew that the poor Mrs. Pickle had lost her family in some tragic way, and that she was happy to have a means to occupy her time and fill her broken heart.

And so it went for many years while Rapunzel grew and flourished under the care of those doting women. Mrs. Tiddlebottom stuffed her with treats and smothered her with kisses at every opportunity, and Mrs. Pickle saw to her meals, baths, and daily excursions through the wildflower fields—always careful not to venture too far away from home, else

Lady Gothel would become anxious. And every day, like clockwork, Gothel would swoop in on the child once nightly before her bedtime to sing her a song and brush her hair, and then she would go directly back into the cellar, where she would spend her nights.

If it hadn't been for the child, Mrs. Tiddlebottom likely would have left the household. Her mistress had become so peculiar, and she was so artificial when she spoke to the child, calling herself Mother, singing that same song, and never calling the girl by her name, always calling her "my flower." It was all too odd for Mrs. Tiddlebottom, all too morbid. She couldn't help wondering how Rapunzel's parents had felt, how they must have missed their little girl, but she didn't dare bring it up to Gothel, who by the year resembled her sisters, Ruby, Martha, and Lucinda, more than ever.

Gothel had taken to wearing her hair in ring-lets and painting her face the way she remembered seeing those odd sisters of hers painting theirs on their last visit. It was as if she was trying to conjure them by dressing like them. A form of sympathetic magic. Gothel went on and on about bringing her sisters back when she saw fit to speak with Mrs. Tiddlebottom at all, which brought Mrs. Tiddlebottom nothing but confusion and vexation. But she decided to keep her thoughts to herself and focus her energy on giving little Rapunzel all the love and care she deserved, because she surely wasn't getting it from her supposed mother.

Mrs. Tiddlebottom felt more than ever that she was an old woman trapped within a fairy tale, and the last thing she wanted was to end up hanging on a rusty hook in the bloody chamber. Or in a cellar.

And the very last thing she wanted was her head to end up in a bell jar.

No, that wouldn't do, not at all. Not for Mrs. Tiddlebottom.

CHAPTER XXVI

THREE MORE FOR CAKE

The years flew by at a manic pace. It seemed like only yesterday that Lady Gothel had brought the baby Rapunzel home, but before they knew it, Mrs. Tiddlebottom and Mrs. Pickle were preparing for Rapunzel's eighth birthday celebration.

"Can you believe our little girl is turning eight?" asked Mrs. Tiddlebottom.

Mrs. Pickle was busily wrapping Rapunzel's gifts. "Yes, our flower has blossomed so quickly! I can hardly believe it!" she said, not realizing Gothel had just walked into the kitchen.

"She is *my flower*, Mrs. P! Mine! And don't you forget it!"

Mrs. Pickle flinched, refusing to make eye contact with Gothel. "Yes, my lady," she said, keeping her eyes on her wrapping.

"And where is my little flower?" asked Gothel. She looked no older than when she and Mrs. Tiddlebottom had first met.

"She's in the wildflower field," said Mrs. Tiddlebottom as she was decorating Rapunzel's birthday cake. "I've asked her to stay out of the kitchen while we make ready for her party."

"Well, you might want to add another layer to that cake, Mrs. T. It seems we will be expecting three more guests this evening. And you know how much my sisters like cake!"

Mrs. Tiddlebottom sighed.

"Do you have an objection to my inviting my sisters to celebrate my daughter's birthday, Mrs. Tiddlebottom?" Gothel asked with a false smile and a singsong cadence to her voice.

"No, Lady Gothel. None whatsoever."

"Very good," said Gothel, exiting the room and leaving the ladies awestruck.

"Did you see what she was wearing?" asked Mrs. Pickle after Gothel left the room.

"Oh, I did. It used to break my heart seeing her dressed like those horrible sisters of hers. Now it just angers me. How dare she invite them here after everything they've done to her? Here! To this house with that young girl here! She is no kind of mother!"

"Shhh! Don't say that so loud!" said Mrs. Pickle, looking to see if Gothel was still about.

"I'm not afraid of her!" said Mrs. Tiddlebottom, slamming her hand on the table, causing the flour to billow and get all over her flower-patterned apron.

"Aren't you? I know I am! And I'm even more afraid of those sisters of hers, if you want to know the truth! From everything you've said, they sound like the stuff of nightmares."

"And so we are!" said someone outside the open window. "We are the stuff of nightmares, and don't you forget it!"

A chill went through the ladies as they saw the odd sisters peering ominously in at them through the kitchen window.

"So, what's this? Mutiny?" asked Lucinda as she and her sisters made their way through the kitchen door.

Mrs. Tiddlebottom's heart almost stopped.

"Calm yourself, old woman! We don't want you keeling over before you're done making that beautiful cake!" said Lucinda.

"No, we couldn't have that!" Ruby laughed. "That would be a shame!"

"Yes, I am so looking forward to having a slice of birthday cake!" said Martha.

"When was the last time we had birthday cake? Was it at Maleficent's birthday?" asked Ruby.

"No, no! We didn't have cake that day! It was all ruined. All destroyed. The stars were right! There was no cake! No cake for Maleficent! No cake for any of us!" said Martha, stamping her feet like a child having a tantrum.

The sisters were more frightening than Mrs. Pickle had imagined.

"Oh, you have no idea!" said Lucinda, laughing.

"And who is this? Mrs. Pickle, is it? What a

strange name. I'm sure it should mean something, but I honestly don't care."

The sisters laughed and laughed, horrifying Mrs. Pickle and Mrs. Tiddlebottom.

"Sisters! You're here!" said Gothel as she made her way into the kitchen, her arms outstretched. She was wearing the same dress as the odd sisters. It was uncanny to see the four of them with their matching dark ringlets, pale faces, tiny red lips, and pink circles painted on their cheeks, all of them looking like terrifying marionettes. Mrs. Tiddlebottom could tell the odd sisters were in shock from seeing Gothel dressed like that.

"Gothel. Hello!" said Lucinda, hardly knowing what else to say.

"Oh!"

"How . . ."

"Oh! I saw you in your mirror. The one you left here. The one you thought to pass off as my mother's so you could spy on me," said Gothel to the confused odd sisters.

"You gave Gothel one of our mirrors?" yelled

Ruby. "Stop giving away all our treasures, Lucinda!"

"We did no such thing, Gothel!" said Lucinda. "I left it as a gift. It was a way for you to contact us when you saw fit to do so."

"Then why hide it among my mother's things? No matter! I treasure it! Let's not dwell in the past! I'm so happy to have my sisters back at last!"

The odd sisters were speechless. They couldn't quite get over her being dressed like them. And they weren't entirely sure why she had invited them.

"I have so much to show you! So much to tell you! You won't believe the progress I've made!" said Gothel like an excited child sharing a favored piece of artwork with her parents.

"We, uh, can't wait to see it," said Lucinda, wondering if they had made the right decision in coming to see Gothel.

"Come with me! Come now!" said Gothel, dragging the sisters toward the cellar door.

"What about the birthday girl?" said Martha, looking around, trying to spy her.

"What about her?" snapped Gothel. "What do

you want with her?" Gothel's face transformed into something monstrous.

"We just wanted to wish her a happy birthday, that is all. It can wait!" said Ruby.

"Yes, it can wait!" said Gothel, smiling at the odd sisters.

"Oh yes! Let's wait! Show us what you're so excited about, Gothel," said Lucinda, letting Gothel lead them down to the cellar.

Mrs. Tiddlebottom found it amusing to see the odd sisters so frightened of Gothel. She wondered what it was they knew about her that caused such fear. Then again, Mrs. Tiddlebottom didn't know much, and everything within her was telling her to leave the house at once. And she would have if it weren't for Rapunzel. She couldn't leave her little girl alone with those witches. Because surely that was what they were.

Witches.

And everyone knew what witches did to children in fairy tales. The last thing Mrs. Tiddlebottom wanted was to see Rapunzel cut up into little pieces and baked in a pie. Or put into a long deathlike sleep. Or into some witch's oven.

Or locked away in a tower. Or even kissed by some prince taking far too many liberties with a sleeping princess.

Nope, Mrs. Tiddlebottom was going to stay put. Her Rapunzel needed her. Even as old as she was, she would protect the girl with everything she had.

"Rapunzel! Come inside, will you?" the old woman called out the back door.

Mrs. Tiddlebottom smiled, seeing her sweet girl run in from the field of wildflowers.

"There's my girl. Here, you look a mess. Let me brush that long unruly hair of yours. I wish your mother would let me cut it for you. Never mind, you are going to look lovely for your birthday!"

Chapter XXVII

The Flower's
Eighth Birthday

Mrs. Tiddlebottom had outdone herself. She'd made an eight-tiered birthday cake covered in delicate marzipan flowers and colorful animals. It was an edible menagerie that rivaled even the famous confections concocted by Mr. Butterpants of Butterpants Bakery. It was a grand spectacle of a cake. A masterpiece. It was the most beautiful cake Mrs. Tiddlebottom had ever seen, if she did say so herself. She was exceedingly proud of that cake and hoped Rapunzel would love it as much as Mrs. Tiddlebottom loved Rapunzel.

The cake was placed on a long table in the front parlor and surrounded by a heap of gifts wrapped in gold paper with pink iridescent ribbons. Mrs. Pickle had made a lovely banner that read HAPPY BIRTHDAY, RAPUNZEL! And the room was decorated with red paper hearts and yellow tissue paper flowers. The only thing missing was Lady Gothel and her sisters.

"By Hades, these madwomen are vexing me to utter distraction!" Mrs. Tiddlebottom had half a mind to pound on the cellar door and command the witches to come out at once.

In all the years she'd lived in that house, she had never gone down to the cellar. Even in the first months after Gothel's return, when she'd started to sequester herself away, leaving poor Mrs. Tiddlebottom to care for the baby Rapunzel alone, she never even knocked at the door. She just let her mistress be. So she wasn't about to knock on the door now, even though she was annoyed they hadn't come up so they could start the celebration.

"Mrs. Tiddlebottom!"

It was Mrs. Pickle. She was in a panic. Her face was red and she was wringing her apron.

"What is it that has you strangling your apron, girl?" Mrs. Tiddlebottom said.

And for a moment Mrs. Pickle forgot all about Rapunzel. "Mrs. T! What's happened to you?"

"What in fairy wings are you talking about, girl?" asked Mrs. Tiddlebottom, becoming annoyed.

"Well, look at you!" she said.

"Oh yes, I probably have flour all over my face, as usual. Now what's got you so upset? Get on with it!"

"No, Mrs. T! Look in the mirror! Something's happened," Mrs. Pickle said, pointing to the oval mirror that hung on the far wall of the parlor. "Go! Look! Right now."

"Good grief!" said Mrs. Tiddlebottom as she made her way to the mirror. "I will if only you'll stop this carrying on." But her tone changed when she saw her reflection. "Oh my!" She couldn't believe her eyes. She was young. It had been so long since she had seen that version of her face she almost didn't recognize it. She just stood there, staring at herself in disbelief.

"Oh, Mrs. Tiddlebottom! The reason I came to find you . . ."

"Yes, child, what is it?" she asked, still looking at herself.

"I can't find Rapunzel! She's not in her room, and she's not outside!"

"What? Are you sure?" Mrs. Tiddlebottom asked, whipping her head around to look at Mrs. Pickle.

"Yes, I've looked all over."

"Rapunzel?" called Mrs. Tiddlebottom. "Where are you, girl?"

"She's nowhere to be found! You don't think she's downstairs with the mistresses, do you?"

"Oh, I hope not!" said Mrs. Tiddlebottom, rushing to the cellar door.

She flung open the door in a panic. "Rapunzel?" The girl didn't answer. Neither did the witches. All she heard were the soft monotone sounds of the witches reciting some sort of song or poem. Mrs. Tiddlebottom couldn't make out the words, but she could hear their voices growing louder each time they recited the poem again. She called down to the witches. "Ladies, I'm sorry to interrupt, but I can't find Rapunzel." Still no answer from the witches. It was eerie, like she was in a dream, calling out for help, but no one could hear her. She went down the first few steps, each of them creaking and moaning as she went. The sounds of the witches' voices became louder. It was a dank, musty place. *It smells of evil down here.* She hardly knew what she would find when she got to the bottom of the stairs, only taking a few at a time, hoping she could see what was happening from a distance. "Mrs. Tiddlebottom! Don't go down there alone!" She started at Mrs. Pickle's voice. "You about made me jump out of my skin! Shhh! If you're coming with me, then keep quiet!" The ladies descended the stairs, slowing. The voices of the witches became cacophonous, hurting their ears.

Then they heard them: the evil words. Even though it was strangely beautiful, something about the song struck fear into Mrs. Tiddlebottom's heart. She knew something foul was happening to her little Rapunzel.

The Flower's Eighth Birthday

Flower, gleam and glow
Let your power shine
Make the clock reverse
Bring back what once was mine

Heal what has been hurt
Change the fates' design
Save what has been lost
Bring back what once was mine

What once was mine

Mrs. Tiddlebottom rushed down the stairs. She couldn't have imagined a more horrific scene. The four witches were in a semicircle, their bloodied hands linked and dripping on Rapunzel's sleeping body. The witches' eyes were rolled back into their heads, and in front of them were three bodies. Two beautiful dead young women and Rapunzel sleeping between, with her long hair brushed out and blanketing the dead beauties.

Her hair glowed as the witches sang their song,

which seemed to be penetrating the dead and lovely creatures:

Flower, gleam and glow
Let your power shine
Make the clock reverse
Bring back what once was mine

Heal what has been hurt
Change the fates' design
Save what has been lost
Bring back what once was mine

What once was mine

Mrs. Pickle screamed, drawing the witches out of their trance. Nothing about the scene was natural, especially the contortions of the witches' faces after being brought of their trace. They were stupefied, and their bodies were twisting in ways that didn't seem possible—in ways that brought terror to Mrs. Tiddlebottom. It was as if something within them were breaking, snapping, causing the witches to cry out in pain. Their peals of horrific screams were like the things of nightmares, but nothing—nothing— was more unimaginable than the image of poor Rapunzel lying there among those dead things as if dead herself.

Gothel's mouth bubbled with black goop as she struggled to spit out her words. "Look what you have done! You fool! You've ruined it!"

"What have you done to Rapunzel?" screamed Mrs. Tiddlebottom.

Lucinda waved her hand at Mrs. Tiddlebottom, causing her to fly backward and smash into a shelf covered in books and glass bottles, which tumbled down on the poor unconscious woman.

Gothel waved her away. "No, Lucinda, no! Don't hurt her!"

Lucinda gave Gothel a queer look. "Why not, Sister? She ruined our spell! She deserves to die!"

"I want her to live. I need her," she said, looking at Mrs. Tiddlebottom's young face, no longer marred by deep lines.

"And what about this one?" asked Lucinda, pointing to Mrs. Pickle, who was huddled in the corner, crying.

"Oh, you can kill her," said Gothel. "She is nothing to me."

"Very good," said Lucinda, laughing. "Sisters. You heard Gothel. Take care of this simpleton while I wipe Mrs. Tiddlebottom's memory."

CHAPTER XXVIII

LET THE WITCHES
EAT CAKE

Gothel and the odd sisters locked the cellar door, hiding away all their secrets from prying eyes while they got up to their skullduggery. Rapunzel was still in an enchanted sleep and wouldn't wake until the odd sisters chose to wake her. Mrs. Tiddlebottom was spirited out of the cellar and up to her room after they altered her memory. Then the foul witches quickly hid all Rapunzel's things. They ripped down her birthday banner and haphazardly packed up all her belongings, stuffing them into the cellar along with everything else they didn't want Mrs. Tiddlebottom to happen upon.

Lucinda performed a remarkable memory charm

that caused Mrs. Tiddlebottom to forget everything that had happened after the soldiers came to take the flower. She wouldn't remember Gothel's leaving, bringing the baby Rapunzel home, or having employed Mrs. Pickle, who had the misfortune of setting foot in such a wicked and demented household. The poor dear's body was still lying on the cellar floor, locked away with the rest of the horrors lurking down there.

Rapunzel became just another possession. An implement to bring Gothel's sisters back from the dead. A way to stay young forever. She wasn't even a person in Gothel's mind. Gothel only saw the flower.

The witches were looking forward to a long afternoon without interruption so they could devise their plans and go over what they should do differently the next time they performed the spell, but suddenly and with great surprise, Mrs. Tiddlebottom wandered into the parlor, looking quite disheveled and worse for wear. She was confused at finding Gothel and the odd sisters stuffing birthday cake into their mouths at an alarming rate.

"Oh, hello, Mrs. Tiddlebottom! What are you doing out of bed?" asked Gothel, annoyed but pretending to be concerned about the poor woman.

"Oh, Mrs. Tiddlebottom, this is a magnificent cake!" squealed Ruby, spitting cake as she spoke.

"Oh, yes, you should try it!" said Lucinda, biting the head off a marzipan kitten.

"Lady Gothel, may I speak with you in the kitchen?" asked Mrs. Tiddlebottom, befuddled and horrified by the entire scene.

"Yes, of course, Mrs. T."

Gothel followed the bemused Mrs. Tiddlebottom into the kitchen. She could see she was confused and probably a little featherheaded. "I'm surprised you're awake, Mrs. T! You were quite woozy after your fall. I think you should go back to bed."

"My fall, lady?"

"Oh dear, you don't remember! You fell down the cellar stairs. I was so worried about you. I still am! Now, please, let's go back upstairs."

"The cellar, lady? I never go into the cellar."

"I know, Mrs. T. I was just as surprised as you are. I think you were looking for me."

"What are your sisters doing here? And why are you dressed that like?" asked Mrs. Tiddlebottom.

"Oh, I'm so sorry, Mrs. T. I hadn't the opportunity to tell you I made peace with my sisters and asked them over for my birthday."

"Your birthday? Oh, Lady Gothel, I didn't know, or I would have baked you a cake!"

"Not to worry, Mrs. T. You've not been well. As you can see, Mr. Butterpants made me a lovely cake. You can bake one for me next time!"

"I feel so strange, lady. Maybe I should go back to bed?"

"Yes, Mrs. T. I think that might be for the best. You've had a very trying day."

"Have I, lady?"

"Well, with being so unwell, I mean."

"Yes."

"I will bring up some tea in a little while, and a slice of Mr. Butterpants's cake?"

"Yes please."

Mrs. Tiddlebottom followed Gothel back to the parlor on her way up to her room and stopped abruptly. She stared into the parlor, dazed. Transfixed. She seemed to be looking for something. She didn't even notice the odd sisters hovering over the cake, devouring it like wild beasts.

"What is it, Mrs. Tiddlebottom?" asked Gothel.

"I'm not sure. Something doesn't feel right, like something is missing."

"There, there, Mrs. Tiddlebottom. Look at all these gifts my sisters brought for me for my birthday!"

"Very nice of them, lady."

"Yes, now go upstairs, and I will be there soon with some tea."

After Gothel saw Mrs. Tiddlebottom disappear up the stairs, she gave the odd sisters a wrathful look.

"What in Hades are you doing to that cake?"

The odd sisters all stopped eating at once and looked at Gothel with the most confused and surprised expressions on their faces.

"What?"

"We have to conduct ourselves as normally as possible! And we have to make that woman up there believe we like her."

"That's stupid. Let's just kill her," said Ruby.

"No! I need her. I'm taking Rapunzel somewhere safe. Somewhere no one can find her. It was stupid of me to think I could keep her here. She's always running about in those fields. Someone is going to happen by one day, and they will put it together and guess she is the missing princess. I've been very sloppy to let this go on so long. No, we need to hide my precious flower away, so no one ever gets their hands on her."

"Then why do you need the old woman?" asked all three of the sisters at once.

"I need someone to watch over my sisters while I'm with Rapunzel," said Gothel, looking at them like they were idiots for not realizing that themselves.

"Oh, and, Lucinda, I will need you to do a memory charm on Rapunzel. Wipe her memory of this place. I want her to think she's always lived in her tower, with me as her doting mother. The only person in the world who loves her."

"And what about her aunties?"

"Best we don't introduce you just yet. I'll have a hard enough time convincing the little brat that I love her."

"Why bother with the pretense at all? Why not just wipe her memory and keep her asleep?" asked Lucinda.

"Oh yes! I love that idea! Yes. Let's keep her asleep! I can't stand the idea of having to spend my days entertaining the little brat!"

"Yes, then it's all set. We'll keep Rapunzel asleep in her tower!" said Ruby, clapping her hands and then stuffing more cake into her mouth.

"And her hair will grow and grow!" said Martha.

"Yes! It will grow so long we will wrap it around your sisters and heal them!" said Lucinda.

"Do you think that will work?" asked Gothel, her eyes wide.

"We do!" the odd sisters said together. It sounded like the clamor of freakish blackbirds.

"Imagine how long her hair will be in ten years!"

Gothel and the odd sisters laughed and laughed. Their cackling rang out into the many kingdoms. They didn't care who or what heard them. As far as anyone knew, they were just four happy sisters eating cake.

Chapter XXIX

The Tower

The tower was hidden away in a valley with a lovely waterfall and surrounded by mountains and a river on three sides. Though low in the valley, it was often drenched in sunlight, and the lands were bursting with greenery. It was a happy tranquil place, an unlikely hiding spot for the queen of the dead, but that was exactly what it had been very long ago. Gothel had learned about the tower in one of her mother's journals. It wasn't far from the dead woods, which now stood in ruins and were completely deserted, considered to be haunted. Haunted by the old queen of the dead and her many minions. Wild tales spread throughout the surrounding lands and became more elaborate as the years passed. It was still a mystery how the soldiers had been able to breach the enchanted thicket all those years ago. It was rumored that the King had employed a very powerful witch to break the enchantment, but to that day the sordid tale was still veiled in mystery and speculation. Gothel hadn't even thought of the enchantment at the time. She just took Jacob's advice and fled. She wondered what would have happened to her and her sisters if she had insisted the soldiers wouldn't be able to enter. She wondered a lot of things.

But that was another lifetime ago, she thought.

Gothel sighed. This was her life now. Traveling between the tower and her country house. Checking on the sleeping Rapunzel and then going back home to check on her sisters. Back and forth. Hither and thither, never staying in either place for long. If she had, she would have had time to think about the ruins of her life and how she'd failed her sisters. Now her entire focus was on bringing them back to life—and keeping herself young so she could.

Even though the odd sisters had given Gothel an enchanted mirror for the tower and one for her pocket, she still made the trip to see that her flower was safe and to use the healing powers to keep herself young. She still resented the Queen for having eaten the flower when she was ill and doing the same when she feared for the life of her unborn child. *Stupid woman.* Gothel wouldn't have had to take their child if the Queen had just used the flower properly, but now the child was infused with the flower's magic and was the only living source of its power. It had been almost ten years since Gothel and the odd sisters brought Rapunzel and her pet, Pascal, to the tower. These days Gothel couldn't go for long without using the flower. Within a day, she would start to age dramatically. She had no idea how the odd sisters stayed so young without the help of the flower, and wondered if they had actually taken her mother's blood, like she had suspected so many years ago.

Rapunzel and Pascal were living in a dream-world created by the odd sisters, in which the

Princess spent her days painting a beautiful mural with paints, made from white seashells, that her mother thoughtfully procured for her from far-off places. She played hide-and-seek with Pascal, did her chores like a good daughter, read stories, played music, baked pies, brushed her exceedingly long hair, did puzzles, and baked even more pies. She filled her days with frivolity and distractions. It was a happy sort of life.

For the most part.

As the years passed in the real world, Gothel saw the mural on the wall growing, becoming more elaborate. As Rapunzel painted it in her dream, it appeared in reality on the walls, filling the tower with Rapunzel's hopes and aspirations. The odd sisters' enchantments made her dreams a reality, and the odd sisters gave Rapunzel free will within her dreams to do and feel and think as she pleased—including a desire to see the lights that appeared in the sky on her birthday.

Which concerned Gothel.

If the dream isn't real, the dreamer finds a way out,

Lucinda had said when Gothel asked why Rapunzel should know about the lanterns that were released every year on her birthday. Gothel took Lucinda's word. She was, after all, a very powerful witch and knew more about those things than Gothel did. The years dragged on as Rapunzel slept, and Rapunzel's mural took up more space until there was no room left in which to paint. There wasn't a wall that wasn't splashed with color, with the young girl's wish for a life of her own. And every time Gothel went back to the tower and saw a new addition to the mural, it sent terror through her soul.

This day was no different. Gothel tethered her horse on the edge of the dead woods. No one dared to go to the dead woods; even now, after all those years, the ruins stood undisturbed. For all she knew, she might be one of its many specters. And in a sense, she was. As she made her way to the tower, one thought consumed her mind.

Tomorrow is Rapunzel's birthday. It's almost been ten years!

And during those years her hair had grown longer and longer.

Long enough to bring Gothel's sisters back from the dead.

Gothel intended to go in through her secret entrance at the tower. This visit wouldn't be like the others—a quick song for Rapunzel to make herself young again and right back to her sisters. This time she'd stay and make the preparations for the ceremony while she waited for the odd sisters to take Primrose's and Hazel's bodies in their flying house to the tower.

Gothel stopped on the path leading to the cave entrance that took her to the valley where the tower was located. She took her hand mirror out of her pocket.

"Show me the sisters!" she said while looking into the mirror. Her face was worn and her hair was starting to gray. Within a few hours, she would be withered.

"Yes, Gothel?" said Lucinda from the mirror.

"Tomorrow is the flower's birthday," said Gothel, almost giddy.

"Yes, we know, Gothel," said Lucinda. Gothel didn't understand why Lucinda seemed so unaffected by something they'd all been waiting for.

"We agreed to do the ceremony again in ten years' time! I need your help!"

"Gothel, we can't help you. We're trapped in the dreamscape!"

"What? Why? How did it happen?" asked Gothel, panicked. She didn't even fully understand how the dreamscape worked. "You can't get out?"

"No. Not even Circe can break the evil fairy's spell!"

"What am I going to do?" Gothel said over and over, paying little mind to Lucinda's confused look and not even bothering to ask how they were.

"What is *she* going to do?" "What is *she* going to do?" Gothel could hear Ruby and Martha in the background before Lucinda answered. "Sisters, quiet! I have something very important to tell Gothel."

All the sisters laughed. "Yes, Lucinda! Tell her! Tell her!"

"What is it?" snapped Gothel, already annoyed with the odd sisters.

"Well, Gothel, you should know, the sleeping spell we put on Rapunzel is broken. She is awake," Lucinda said from her magic mirror with a wicked look of satisfaction on her face.

"Awake? How? How do you know?" Gothel said, straining to see her up in the tower through the cave.

"We see everything, Gothel. She thinks it's just like any other day. The day her mother comes home with the shopping. But today she plans to ask you if she can finally go see the lights that appear in the sky every year on her birthday."

"I told you we shouldn't have included that in her dream, you stupid witch!" snapped Gothel.

"Don't you snap at me, old woman!" screeched Lucinda.

"How dare you!" screamed Gothel.

"How dare us? How dare us? Did you let us use your little flower to heal our friend? No! You hoarded it! You threw us out of your house!"

"But I promised to give the girl to you once I was finished with her! I promised you could do with her what you would as soon as my sisters were brought back! Don't do this! What will Circe think of your meddling with another princess?"

"Well, it's too late for all that now, Gothel. Maleficent is dead, and we may be trapped in the dreamscape forever if Circe doesn't stop being angry with us. So now you can deal with this on your own!"

You are destined to be alone, Gothel! Her mother's words rang in her ears.

Gothel took a deep breath. "I will! I will deal with Rapunzel and wake my sisters on my own! Watch from your mirror if you'd like, and see for yourself." Gothel almost chucked the mirror in anger.

"Yeah, good luck with that. And by the way, I don't think Circe will mind if my sisters and I help the missing princess," said Lucinda, cackling before the mirror turned black.

Gothel grumbled as she made her way to the

tower. "Gods! I'm going to have to actually talk to this girl! What are we going to talk about?"

She heard the odd sisters laughing from the mirror in her pocket. "So this is how I'm to spend my days. In torment of these impossible witches and making a pretense of being this girl's mother?"

Gothel ignored the sisters and kept grumbling to herself. "Okay, okay. Rapunzel thinks this is just any other day. You can do this, Gothel. You can make this brat believe you're her mother. Just pretend you like her. After all, you are her mother. The only mother she has ever known."

Finally, she reached the tower. She stood beneath the open window and called up to her flower, trying her best to sound sweet. Trying to act like this was any other day in Rapunzel's dream life. She needed to sound like a mother. She needed to sound convincing. She needed to sound real.

"Rapunzel! Let down your hair!" She hated the way her voice sounded even as she was saying the words.

"Rapunzel, I'm not getting any younger down here!" she sang out.

"Coming, Mother!" called Rapunzel from the tower. Gothel could hear the odd sisters laughing again from the mirror in her pocket.

"Shut up, you stupid witches! She's coming!" Gothel gasped when she saw Rapunzel's hair cascade down the tower. It was longer than she'd thought, longer than it had looked when it was gathered around her while she slept.

Long enough to wrap around my sisters and bring them back to life!

CHAPTER XXX

ODD SISTERS
KNOW BEST

In the land of dreams, things were chaotic and unpredictable, yet there was a rhythm to the place if you were cunning enough to find it. And for those who found it and learned to harness the magic, almost anything was possible in the dreamscape. Each inhabitant of the dreamscape lived within his or her own chamber composed of tall mirrors, each of them reflecting different images showing the dreamer events from the outside world connected to the dreamer. Some dreamers simply sat and watched the events pass by, while others learned how to control the mirrors and command what they saw in the mirrors. The odd sisters, who were already well versed in mirror magic, had no problem mastering the mirrors in the dreamworld. They found the rhythm. They harnessed the magic. For them almost anything was possible. And that was how they were able to watch Gothel.

They saw Gothel and Rapunzel standing in front of a large mirror in their tower. "Oh, look, Sisters. She's there!" said Lucinda.

Ruby and Martha clapped their hands, stomping their feet. "Oh, let's see what kind of mother she makes!"

"Shhh! Look! I think she's saying something to us in the mirror!" said Lucinda, pointing at the image of Gothel and Rapunzel reflected at them in the dreamscape.

"Rapunzel, look in that mirror. You know what I see? I see a strong, confident, beautiful young lady!" Gothel *was smiling at her own reflection and then said, "Oh, look! You're there, too!"*

The odd sisters shook their heads. "She isn't acting at all like the mother Rapunzel knew from her dream," said Martha.

"We didn't tell her to," Lucinda said, laughing.

"Shhh! Listen! They're talking!"

"No, no, no, can't be. I distinctly remember, your birthday was last year." The odd sisters laughed as Gothel tried to pretend it wasn't Rapunzel's birthday.

"That's the funny thing about birthdays, they're kind of an annual thing." Rapunzel sighed and went on. *"Mother, I'm turning eighteen, and I wanted to ask, uh, what I really want for this birthday . . . Actually, what I've wanted for quite a few birthdays . . ."*

"Spit it out, dear!" yelled Ruby at the mirror as she watched the poor girl struggling to find the words.

"Okay, Rapunzel, please stop with the mumbling. Blah-blah-blah-blah, it's very annoying," said Gothel.

"She couldn't act like a mother if she tried!" said Martha.

"This is even better than I thought it would be!" said Ruby, laughing so hard she fell to the floor and rolled around in fits. Soon Martha joined her, and the two were laughing so hard they were crying, causing their makeup to drip down their hysterical faces.

"Sisters! Sisters, please! Stop this!" screamed

Lucinda. But her sisters couldn't stop laughing at Gothel's ridiculous mother act.

"You're missing the entire thing, Sisters!" yelled Lucinda. "She's singing a song, for goodness' sake!" But her sisters couldn't stop rolling around on the floor, laughing so hard the mirrors in their chamber were shaking.

"What would Circe think if she saw you now? Ruby! Martha! Stop this at once!" Immediately the sisters stopped.

"No fair conjuring Circe!" said Ruby, tears still running down her face.

"I didn't summon her. I'm just reminding you that we need to conduct ourselves properly if we want to ever be let out of this place!"

"Did I hear you say Gothel sang a song?" asked Ruby, trying to muffle her laughter.

"You missed it. The girl asked to see the lights, and Gothel pranced around the tower like a chicken, singing of the terrors and dangers outside the tower." Lucinda couldn't even keep a straight face while she tried to recount the story. "Just shut up and listen," she said, trying to keep herself from laughing. "Gothel is saying something else."

"Don't ever ask to leave this tower again."

The sisters fell into peals of laughter again. "Don't ever ask to leave the tower again!" Ruby screamed. "Does Gothel really think that is going to work?"

"She's an eighteen-year-old girl!" said Martha. "Of course it won't work!"

"Oh, Rapunzel, I love you more!" mocked Martha.

"I love you most?" Lucinda laughed. "Princesses may be stupid, but I don't think Rapunzel is stupid enough to believe that!"

"Where do you think Gothel is going?" screeched Ruby. "She's leaving the girl alone!"

"Follow her in the mirrors," said Lucinda. "I will keep an eye on the girl."

Ruby went to one of the other mirrors and watched Gothel wander the forest. Lucinda kept an eye on Rapunzel. She almost preferred the dream-scape to the real world, with so many mirrors at her disposal. Sometimes you saw things within the mirrors of the dreamscape you didn't even know you wanted to see until they appeared before you.

The sisters saw Gothel taking the path that led to the dead forest. "The queen of nothing is headed to her ruined lands."

"Tragic!" screamed Martha.

"She's searching for something," said Lucinda, taking her eyes off Rapunzel for a moment, noticing something in one of the other mirrors. "Sisters, look! It's him!" Lucinda pointed to a mirror that showed a young man going into the cave entrance to the valley. "It's Flynn Rider! He has the crown!"

"Who?" asked Ruby.

"Flynn Rider!" snapped Lucinda.

"What kind of name is that? Flynn Rider?" asked Martha.

"Sisters! Please. He's the young man I told you about," said Lucinda. "Shhh!"

"Ah yes, the one you compelled to take the crown and bring it to Rapunzel!" said Martha.

"Which crown?" asked Ruby.

"For Hades' sake, Ruby! Rapunzel's crown! Remember she's a princess!"

"Yes, yes, yes! There's so many stories to keep track of! So many princesses! Stop getting so annoyed with us!" cried Ruby.

"Lucinda! He's breaking into the tower! He's there!" Martha said, pointing at one of the many mirrors in the chamber.

"Oh! She hit him in the head!" said Ruby, laughing.

"Serves him right, breaking into the tower!" said Martha.

"Martha! Please do keep up! We want Flynn to break into the tower!" Lucinda said, shaking her head.

"Do we?" asked Martha.

"Yes, we do! How else is he to get Rapunzel the crown?" Lucinda walked away from the mirror, more frustrated with her sisters than she'd been in quite some time.

"Oh gods! Look at the way Rapunzel is looking

at him! Why do princesses always fall in love with the first boy they see?" asked Martha.

"Because that's the way fairy tales are written," said Lucinda, sighing.

"Ha! No! She hit him with the pan again! Good girl!" Ruby said, laughing. "She's shoving him in the closet!"

"Sisters, listen! Pay attention, both of you! We want Flynn Rider in the tower! We want them to be friends. We need him to help Rapunzel find her true family again."

"But why?"

"We don't want Gothel to wake her sisters, now, do we?"

"Of course we don't!" Ruby and Martha said.

"Hades! She's on her way back with a sleeping potion! Look!" said Lucinda, pointing at Gothel in one of the mirrors.

"Is it one of ours, Lucinda? One of our sleeping potions?"

"It doesn't matter! Flynn is in that closet, and we need Rapunzel to get rid of Gothel and talk Flynn into taking her to see the lights!"

"Yes! If she doesn't kill him with that frying pan first." The sisters laughed.

"And what about Gothel? What about the sleeping potion? She's going to try to put that girl back to sleep!"

"The girl will have to get rid of her before she tries to use it!"

"Oh! Look! Look! Rapunzel has the crown! She's trying it on! She's trying it on!"

"Let's just tell her now she's the Princess!" squealed Ruby.

"We can't talk to her through the mirror, idiot! She doesn't have magic! And even if we could, I wouldn't want to spoil all the fun of seeing Gothel squirm!" said Lucinda. "I want her to think she's won. I want to fill her heart with hope and then see it destroyed!"

"She's there! Gothel's there! Look!" said Ruby, pointing to one of their mirrors, where Gothel was calling up to the tower window.

"Rapunzel, let down your hair."

"One moment, Mother!" called the Princess after stashing the crown in a vase.

"I have a big surprise for you!" called Gothel

"I have one, too!" said Rapunzel.

"Why has Gothel been using that strange singsong voice? It's ridiculous!" said Ruby.

The odd sisters were transfixed by the images in the mirror as they listened to Gothel's and Rapunzel's voices dancing around each other. Each was too consumed with her own plans to listen to the other.

"My surprise is bigger!" yelled Gothel as Rapunzel pulled her into the tower with her long hair. The odd sisters could see Gothel going in through the window; she was acting very animated, almost like a stage actor, or a large puppet. "I brought back parsnips! I'm going to make hazelnut soup for dinner, your favorite. Surprise!"

The odd sisters laughed. "Soup! That's the surprise?" screeched Martha.

"Hazelnut sleeping-potion soup! *Surprise!*" yelled Ruby, making Martha laugh.

"Well, Mother, there is something I want to tell you," said Rapunzel.

The odd sisters screamed. "No! No! No! Don't tell her!" The girl couldn't hear them, of course, but there was power in their voices, magic, and they were trying to use it to manipulate Rapunzel. "Shhh! Gothel is talking."

"You know I hate leaving you, especially after a fight when I've done absolutely nothing wrong," said Gothel. The sisters laughed. She had no idea how to act like a mother. She'd never taken care of the child when Rapunzel was little.

"Whatever happened to Mrs. Tiddlebottom?" asked Ruby. And suddenly Mrs. Tiddlebottom appeared in one of the mirrors. She was baking a magnificent cake, bigger and more beautiful than the one she had made for Rapunzel's eighth birthday.

"Stop it! We're supposed to be watching Gothel! Get rid of Mrs. Tiddlepants!"

"Tiddlebottom!"

"What?"

"Her name is Tiddlebottom!"

"Well, frankly I think both names are ludicrous!" Lucinda snapped.

"Is she baking a cake for Rapunzel? Does she remember her?"

"Not quite," said Lucinda. "But something compels her to make a cake every year on this day. Shhh! Never mind her and listen. I think that stupid girl is about to tell Gothel Flynn is in the closet!"

"Enough with the lights, Rapunzel!" yelled Gothel. "You are not leaving this tower ever!"

"Oh! Look at Gothel showing her true colors!" Ruby said. "There's the Gothel we know!"

Gothel reclined on the nearest chair dramatically as if yelling had drained her. "She's really hamming it up!" said Ruby, giggling as she watched Gothel put her hand on her head as if she were going to faint from the exhaustion of it all.

"This is too much!" said Ruby. "Like a badly acted melodrama!"

"Agh! Great! Now I'm the bad guy," declared Gothel, exasperated with Rapunzel and tired of the pretense.

The odd sisters knew Gothel wanted to put Rapunzel to sleep so she could take Rapunzel's body back to her country house and wake her sisters. And as much as it delighted the odd sisters to think of the macabre scene of Gothel wrapping that young girl's hair around her dead sisters, they weren't about to put another princess in danger. Not while Circe was watching their every move. If they hurt one more silly princess, then Circe would never let them out of the dreamscape. And they would never see their Circe again.

"All I was going to say was I know what I want for my birthday now," said Rapunzel.

"And what is that?" asked Gothel, annoyed with the entire charade.

"New paint. The paint made from the white shells you once brought me."

"That is a very long trip, Rapunzel. Almost three days' time."

"Long enough to check on your sisters," said Lucinda. "I think there is something wrong with them. You'd better check."

"Yes! You'd better check on your sisters, Gothel!" cried Ruby.

"They're in danger, Gothel! Mrs. Tiddlebottom

must be old now without her flower. So frail. Your sisters aren't safe alone with her," said Lucinda, binding her words with magic, using them to make Gothel afraid.

"Mrs. Tiddlebottom might go down into the cellar! You've never been away this long!" said Martha.

"Go! Go to your sisters!" said the odd sisters at once.

"You're sure you will be all right on your own?" asked Gothel.

"I know I'm safe as long as I'm here," said Rapunzel.

"I'll be back in three days' time," said Gothel as she took the basket Rapunzel had put together for her journey.

"I love you very much, dear," said Gothel.

"I love you more," said Rapunzel.

And she did. The sisters could tell.

Rapunzel actually loved her mother Gothel.

CHAPTER XXXI

BREAK HER HEART, CRUSH HER SOUL

The odd sisters watched Gothel tentatively go through the secret cave exit, to make her way through the dead woods and to her house in the country. "That's right, Gothel. Rapunzel will be fine. Your sisters need you."

They kept their eyes on Rapunzel, who was armed with a frying pan and cautiously approaching the wardrobe, which had been locked tight with a green rocking chair. She quietly moved the chair away from the closet and quickly hid behind it.

"Flynn is in there!" screeched Martha. "She's going to let him out?"

"Of course she's going to let him out! Shhh! Let's see what happens."

"How did she learn to do all these tricks with her hair?" asked Martha, watching Rapunzel use her hair like a lasso to open the wardrobe door.

"We gave her free will in her dream. Everything that happened in the dream translates into real life for her. Now be quiet!"

The sisters laughed and laughed as they saw Flynn Rider fall face-first onto the floor. "Shhh! Sisters! Too loud!" Ruby said. The odd sisters looked around themselves, wondering who they might be bothering and why Ruby cared. "I don't want Gothel to hear us!"

"Gothel can't hear us unless we speak into her mirror! How many times do I have to explain this to you? I swear you two are becoming more feather-headed by the day!"

"Ha! Look! She tied him up!" said Ruby. "And her frog is slapping him to wake him up!"

"It's a chameleon, Ruby. We gave it to her, remember! On her birthday! Shhh, Rapunzel is saying something."

"We gave her a frog for her birthday?"

Lucinda sighed. "Yes. Well, no. We gave her the chameleon on her eighth birthday. Now keep up. For goodness' sake, what's wrong with you!"

"So the frog has been alone all this time in the tower while she slept? What did he do all day?"

"He slept, too! Now shut up!" said Lucinda. "Rapunzel is talking!"

"Struggling, struggling is pointless," said Rapunzel.

"Oh, look at her trying to be brave!" said Lucinda. "Precious."

The odd sisters saw the look of confusion on Flynn Rider's face.

"Is this hair?" he said, trying to find the person the hair belonged to in the darkness.

"Oh, he's a smart one!" said Martha sarcastically. "There's no way we can count on this one to get Rapunzel to the castle. He's useless. Look at him!"

"Sisters, shhh!" scolded Lucinda. "I think she's talked him into taking her to see the lanterns in exchange for the stolen crown."

"But that's her crown!"

"I know! But Rapunzel doesn't know that! He took it from the castle, remember? Keep up!"

"Wait! What? Shhh. Flynn is doing something weird, he's about to say something!" The sisters listened as Flynn Rider spoke ominous words.

"All right, listen, I didn't want to have to do this, but you leave me no choice. Here comes the smolder. . . ."

"Lucinda! What's 'the smolder'? Is it a burning spell? Is he going to kill her?"

"No, dear. His so-called charms aren't magical," said Lucinda, laughing.

"What is he doing with his face? What's he doing with his face?"

The sisters laughed. "He's ridiculous! Like a silly, harmless Gaston!"

The sisters couldn't stop laughing. They were laughing so hard they fell onto the floor again.

When the sisters finally stopped laughing, they realized it had all been decided. Flynn Rider had agreed to take Rapunzel to see the lanterns in exchange for the crown he had stolen.

"He's taking her to the lights! He's taking her to the lights! He's taking her to the lights!" they sang as they danced around their chamber.

"Oh-oh! Let's see what Gothel is doing now!" said Lucinda, directing her attention to one of the other mirrors. "Show us Gothel!" she said, but changed her mind. "No, wait! Look at Rapunzel! She's in the world! And she's worried she is going to break Gothel's heart and crush her soul!"

"Oh please! That's so dramatic!" said Ruby.

"No, those were her words! Crush her soul!"

"And Flynn is trying to talk her into going back to the tower! Horrible man!"

But the sisters were distracted by the mirror they had conjured Gothel within. "What is that horse doing? Lucinda, look there! That horse is attacking Gothel!"

"*A palace horse. Where's your rider?*" said Gothel, *flying into a panic and calling Rapunzel again and again.*

"She's going back to the tower! She's going back to the tower!" squealed Ruby.

The odd sisters watched Gothel as she raced back to the tower. It was dark and empty and full of shadows. "Your precious flower is gone!" screamed the odd sisters. "Gone, gone, gone forever!" they screeched like harpies.

"Now Gothel will know what it's like to lose everything! She will lose her precious flower!" Lucinda said snippily, making Ruby laugh.

Martha got quiet, not joining in the celebration. "What is it, Martha?" asked her sisters.

"But she already has lost everything, hasn't she? She's lost her sisters. She lost her home. And now she's losing the last chance she has to bring her sisters back."

"What are you saying, Martha?" asked Lucinda.

"We should have told her," Martha said in a very small voice, tears running down her face and silencing her cackling sisters.

"And we would have if she hadn't turned on us!" snapped Lucinda. "She wouldn't share the flower! She doesn't deserve to know!"

Martha persisted, surprising her sisters. "We

should have told her the moment we learned! Not waited."

Lucinda shook her head as if trying to banish a terrible thought. "We don't have time to talk about this now. I won't waste my time feeling guilty about Gothel! If it weren't for her, Maleficent might still be alive!"

Martha knew Lucinda was right. "I know, I know." But the conversation was interrupted by a blood-chilling scream. It was Ruby.

"What in Hades has happened, Ruby!"

"Gothel has found the crown! She's found the wanted poster!"

"No matter, my dear sisters. It's all been written."

Ruby nodded at the image in the mirror. "Is the part about Gothel carrying that large knife also written?"

"There is no fear of an unhappy ending for Rapunzel. She is not the victim in this story. That role has already been laid out for Gothel. Oh, her heart will be broken, my precious sisters, and her soul will be crushed. I have seen to that!"

"What do you mean? What do you mean?"

"You'll see, my dears. Let Gothel take her knife and set out into the world. She knows little more of the world than Rapunzel does."

CHAPTER XXXII

MOTHER GOTHEL

"Show me the sisters!" screamed Gothel into her hand mirror. She was expecting to see Lucinda's mocking face looking back at her. Instead she found her sisters—her real sisters. Primrose and Hazel. Their coffins were open.

"What? What's this?" Gothel's heart was racing. "Where's Mrs. Tiddlebottom? Show me Mrs. Tiddlebottom!" she yelled. The mirror showed only her own face. "Show me the old woman!" she screamed.

Lucinda appeared in the mirror, laughing. "You're the old woman, Gothel. Look at yourself. You're dying without the flower. You took that girl from her family, lied to her, and made her think she's your daughter! You've dedicated your life to a lie, just like your mother!"

"Shut up! You know nothing of my mother!"

"We know everything about your mother! Your mother lied to you. You're not her daughter! Not in the way you think! Have you ever heard her talk about a father? No! That's because she created you with magic!"

"Lies!" screamed Gothel.

"No, dear, you're the queen of lies, not I! You and your mother both. Look into your soul, Gothel. The truth is there. She is there." And Gothel knew Lucinda was telling the truth. She'd known it her entire life.

"So what if she did create me with magic? I'm still her daughter!"

"You've always been selfish, Gothel, too concerned with yourself to listen to anyone else! Even your poor sisters, who didn't want the life you had planned. Remember when Manea said you were her? Well, you are! You are your mother in more ways than one! You are her blackhearted daughter, but without any of her majesty, and without any of her powers!"

"And my sisters? What of them?"

Lucinda laughed. "They aren't even your real sisters, Gothel! I mean, come on, look at them! Your mother had Jacob take them from nearby villages. She enchanted them to be what you needed to survive in the dead woods as queen once you took over—Primrose to entertain you, and Hazel to be your heart! But it all went wrong, horribly wrong, and now you're alone."

Lucinda laughed again and continued.

"Look at you! *Mother* Gothel! You're no more of a mother than your own mother was. You're exactly like her. Selfish, cruel, and manipulating, but without any of her ambition, any of her magic! You're pathetic! You've wasted your life. Gods, it's no wonder your mother could hardly stand the sight of you!"

"I don't care if they're not my real sisters! I love them! They're better sisters than you ever were!"

"Do you love them? Do you really?" asked Lucinda. "If you did, then you would have given them your mother's blood and not worried that they would be able to read your mind!"

"I didn't want them to know my heart! I was afraid!"

"If they were your real sisters, they would have already known your heart, as we do."

"You know my heart with magic!"

"What did Primrose say when we tried to bring her and Hazel back to life? What were the words she mustered from beyond the veil?" asked Lucinda.

"'Let us die.'"

"Yes, 'let us die'! Those were her words, and yet you've been trying to find a way to bring them back these many years. She'd rather be dead than live with you, a replica of her foul, murdering mother! A woman who killed children, blinded them, and compelled them to do her bidding! And you condoned it! You thought it was perfectly natural!"

"And so do you! I know you do!"

"You know our hearts, as we know yours. You

see, Gothel, you have been focusing all your love on the wrong sisters. They didn't understand you. Not like we do."

"What do you mean?"

"It's all too late now, Gothel. Go after the flower. Follow your fool's errand and see where that takes you. You will find them at the Snuggly Duckling. Go there quickly before they leave. It's not far from where you are. We see them in our many mirrors. We are watching. Behind the mirrors. Where always are. Where we will always be." And the mirror went black, leaving Gothel alone. Just as her mother had said she would be.

The odd sisters kept watching from the dream-scape. The mirrors were flashing different images at a startling rate, telling them the story—a story they already knew. A story that had been written long before but was only now appearing on the pages of their tome. And they had a feeling their Circe was reading the book as the story unfolded. They had made sure to admonish Gothel. Circe would see. She would see their good deeds and forgive them.

She would let them free. But no matter how hard they tried, they couldn't see Circe. They didn't know where she was or what she was doing. They couldn't see Nanny or the goings-on in Morningstar Kingdom, and they knew it was Circe's doing.

Lucinda looked at the many mirrors and saw Gothel peeking in the window at the Snuggly Ducking.

She's found them, she thought. *This story is almost over.*

Chapter XXXIII

The Snuggly Duckling

The odd sisters watched Gothel spying in the window at the Snuggly Duckling, the foul place Flynn Rider took the flower to in a vain attempt to frighten her. He hoped the place, filled with ruffians and murderers, would make her flee back to her mother and the safety of her tower, and that he would get his crown back without having to take her to see the lanterns. But she didn't run. She rallied the hooligans to her cause; she got the black-guards to help her.

"They're buffoons!" shouted Martha.

"What is this tomfoolery?" Ruby said, laughing.

"Are these supposed to be the bad guys?"

"What is that little man wearing? A diaper? Wings?"

"Clever girl, she's brought them to her side!" said Ruby, clapping her hands and stomping her little boots while spinning in a circle. Lucinda and Martha joined Ruby's dance as they watched the images of Rapunzel and Flynn Rider appear in the mirrors, flashing like lightning. It was terrifying to the witches to watch the events unfold. Palace guards. A maniacal horse. A narrow escape. And then Gothel, talking to the small man with wings outside the tavern door.

"Gothel is going to kill the little man in the diaper!" screeched Ruby.

"Let her! He's obscene!" said Martha.

"No, Sisters. He's just told her where the secret tunnel from the Snuggly Duckling lets out. She's going to find them! She's going to find Rapunzel and Flynn."

"No, she won't!" said Ruby, casting her hand at the mirror.

"What did you do?" yelled Lucinda.

"I made sure they went another way."

"You almost killed them!" shouted Lucinda, watching in horror images flashing before them in their many mirrors.

"But I didn't! They're safe in the cavern."

"Ruby! The cavern is flooded. The dam is broken!"

They watched Rapunzel cry in the flooded cavern. "They're trapped," screamed Martha.

"I'm so sorry, Flynn," said Rapunzel.

"Eugene," he said, correcting her.

"What?"

"My real name is Eugene Fitzherbert. Someone might as well know."

The sisters laughed. "There is no time for flirting, you fools!" Lucinda was screaming into the mirrors. "Are they giving up? Wait, no, listen!"

"I have magic hair that glows when I sing. I have magic hair that glows when I sing!"

"Ah! She's figured out a way out of the cavern!"

"Smart girl! Smart girl!" said Ruby and Martha, dancing in circles and clicking their heels on the floor. "Smart girl!"

"Sisters, shhh! We'd better keep watching to make sure they get to the castle safely. Wait! Look! Gothel is at the duck door!"

"Duck door?"

"The duck door, Ruby! The end of the secret passage from the pub! Never mind! She is talking to those ruffians! Making some sort of deal. She's up to something!"

"Didn't you say it was already written? Why are you worried, Lucinda?"

"It's odd looking into the future, Sisters. Though it is likely to come to pass, what we see isn't always fixed," she said. "So keep your eyes on all the mirrors and tell me if Gothel is up to any more of her trickery!"

Chapter XXXIV

Rapunzel Knows Best

Gothel was watching Rapunzel and Flynn Rider huddled together near a fire. She could see the two were becoming closer, sitting there all cozily together, sharing stories and making eyes at each other.

"Oh gods, this is sickening!" said Gothel, watching the young couple talk. *They are becoming a couple, aren't they?* She had to break the bond between them. She had gone about all of this the wrong way. All of it! Maybe the odd sisters were right.

"Of course we're right!" said the odd sisters from Gothel's hand mirror.

Gothel snatched it out of her pocket and narrowed her eyes at Lucinda. "What do you see in those mirrors? Do you see the future? Do you know how this is going to end? All I want is to bring my sisters back! Please! Just help me. I'll give the girl back to her parents afterwards, I promise!"

The odd sisters laughed. "Maybe if you actually loved Rapunzel, she wouldn't be running away from you now. Maybe if you'd actually raised her and created a real home and life for her, she wouldn't be falling in love with the first boy she met!"

"Oh! The way Circe loves you?" snapped Gothel, her words like a dagger.

"I told you not to mention her name!" said Lucinda in a firm yet surprisingly calm voice that sent a hollow feeling through Gothel.

"What are you going to do about it from the dreamscape?" Gothel snapped, standing her ground.

"Don't forget, Gothel, one of our mirrors is in your cellar—*with your sisters*. Cross the line with us again and you shall see how far our fury can extend!"

"You keep my sisters out of this!"

"And you keep Circe out of it as well," warned Lucinda. "And you'd better look to your flower. It looks like she's falling in love," she added before the mirror went black. Gothel heard Flynn Rider saying he was going to get more wood for their fire. She crept up behind Rapunzel and just stood there a moment, watching her flower in silence. She wondered if Rapunzel could feel her standing there, like a grim specter in the darkness. The way she'd always felt it when her own mother was near.

"Well, I thought he'd never leave," said Gothel, startling Rapunzel.

"Mother?"

"Hello, dear."

"I-I-I don't—how did you find me?"

"Oh, it's easy, really. I just listened to the sound of complete and utter betrayal and followed that."

Rapunzel sighed. "Mother."

"We're going home, Rapunzel. Now."

"You don't understand. I've been on this incredible journey and I've seen and learned so much. I even met someone."

"Yes, the wanted thief. I'm so proud. Come on, Rapunzel."

"Mother, please! I think—I think he likes me."

"Likes you? Please, Rapunzel, that's demented."

"But, Mother, I—"

"This is why you never should have left! Dear, this whole romance that you've invented just proves you're too naive to be here. Why would he like you? Come on now, really! Look at you. You think that he's impressed? Don't be a dummy, come with Mummy. Mother—"

"No!" Rapunzel yelled, finally finding her voice with her mother, finding the courage to stand up to her.

"'No'? Oh. I see how it is. Rapunzel knows best! Rapunzel's so mature now, such a clever grown-up miss. Rapunzel knows best. Fine, if you're so sure now, go ahead and give him this!" said Gothel, handing Rapunzel the satchel with the crown.

"How did you—"

Gothel didn't answer her. She kept ranting. "This is why he's here! Don't let him deceive you! Give it to him. Watch, you'll see!"

"I will!"

"Trust me, my dear," Gothel said, snapping her fingers. "That's how fast he'll leave you. I won't say I told you so—no! Rapunzel knows best! So if he's such a dreamboat, go and put him to the test!"

"Mother, wait!"

"If he's lying, don't come crying! Mother knows best!"

And Gothel left her flower alone, with her doubts and fears. Alone to wonder if Flynn Rider only wanted the crown.

"Yes, my little flower. Give him the crown and find out," said Gothel in the distance as she watched her flower struggling with what to do next.

This time Rapunzel could feel her mother lurking in the distance, but she couldn't see her or the hooligans standing beside her.

"Patience, boys. All good things to those who wait."

CHAPTER XXXV

AT LAST SHE
SEES THE LIGHT

In one of their many mirrors, the odd sisters watched as Rapunzel entered for the first time the kingdom, with its cobblestone paths, elaborate archway entrance, and enormous blue castle nestled on a lush green hillside. The kingdom was a vibrant, beautiful place filled with lovely muted purples and blues. And everywhere Rapunzel looked, there were purple banners splashed with gold stars. There were flower garlands and gingerbread-style cottage store-fronts. It was the most beautiful place Rapunzel had ever seen. There was a magnificent mural on one of the enclaves, where little girls gathered to leave offerings for the lost princess. The mural was of the

King and Queen and their daughter with golden hair. *The lost princess.*

The odd sisters saw Rapunzel dash off before they could help her remember. But they wove a spell to bind her, and spun their words like a web, tangling her within her story—the story of the stolen baby, the Princess who was spirited away from her true family, the little girl without a home until the day the thief brought her back. As they watched the Princess dance in the square, they filled her heart with joy and the overwhelming feeling that she was at home. She had never felt so alive.

And then it was time—time to watch the lights.

It started with one lantern. One lonely and heartbreaking lantern. Rapunzel didn't know why it filled her heart with such sorrow to see it floating alone, reflected in the water, but then the kingdom started to shimmer with thousands of lanterns, and her heart was filled with the same joy she had experienced when she saw the mural of the royal family.

"I think she knows, Lucinda."

"I think there's a spark of it in her heart. I think she almost knows."

"I'm happy we gave the King and Queen the idea to light the lanterns on her birthday," said Lucinda, watching the lights rise into the heavens.

"They've been calling to her. Just as we hoped," said Martha.

"Do you think Circe will blame us for betraying Gothel? For giving the counter enchantment to the King so his guards could get through the thicket?" asked Ruby.

"We did it to get Gothel out of that horrid place. To bring her closer to us! We had no idea it would . . . Never mind. Gothel is lost to us," said Lucinda.

"Look—I think Rapunzel knows." They watched as the young princess experienced more joy than she had known her entire lifetime.

"She will know soon. The spark is turning into a light. Her world has shifted," said Martha, smiling at the Princess surrounded by the floating lights.

"Wait? What is that? That green light?" asked Ruby.

"What green light?" asked Lucinda. "Where?"

"Look, in that mirror. On the shore! Gothel's hooligans!" And then the mirrors went black.

"What's happened?" The sisters were in a panic.

"Show us the girl!" screamed Lucinda, but all the mirrors were cold and still, and eerily dark.

"I don't understand!" said Lucinda, searching all the mirrors and finding only blackness.

"What's wrong with the mirrors? Why have they gone black?"

Then a face appeared in every mirror. It was solemn and filled with wrath.

"Stop interfering!" It was Circe.

"We're helping!" cried the odd sisters. "We're helping the Princess."

"You're not to interfere with anyone ever again. Do you understand?"

"But—"

"It will only end in heartbreak if you do, my sisters, my mothers."

"But—"

"Every time you try to help, something goes

wrong. You are walking nightmares, a menace! Ursula is dead because of you! Maleficent has died by your hands! Snow White is forever plagued by nightmares because you tortured her as a child! You destroy everything you touch! Now please, you've already ruined one life in this story, and I'm afraid she is already beyond redemption. Do you really want to ruin another?"

"But—"

"No! Leave this to me! If you ever want to see me again, you will leave it alone. You will trust that the fairies and I have this handled. Do not interfere!"

"What do you mean you and the fairies?" asked Lucinda.

"I have to go now. Please, for your own sake and mine, don't try to interfere," said Circe, her face completely impassive.

"Can we have our mirrors back?" asked Lucinda.

"Not until the end. You can have your mirrors back at the end."

Circe sighed. "Good-bye, Mothers." And the mirrors went black.

"Our daughter has betrayed us. She is working with the fairies. She's turned her back on us! Giving us ultimatums? Trying to command us! We created her! She is alive because we brought her out of nothing. We gave her the best parts of ourselves, and this is how she repays us?" Lucinda was incensed.

"I don't understand! We were trying to help the Princess," said Ruby.

"Circe doesn't care! She's the fairies' creature now. She belongs to Nanny and the others. She is dead to us. Our enemy."

"No, Lucinda! You don't mean that!"

"She thinks we destroy everything we touch? She thinks we are walking nightmares? She has seen nothing!"

"Lucinda, no! We can't hurt Circe!"

"We won't hurt her, my dear. For hurting her would be like hurting ourselves," said Lucinda, repeating the old words that had been said by many witches who had come before them.

"What are you going to do?"

"We are going to destroy everything she holds

dear. Rip her away from those who fill her head with lies about us. Those who seek to take her from us."

"Won't that make her hate us even more?"

"No, it will bring her closer to us. We will have our Circe again."

CHAPTER XXXVI

BETRAYED

Gothel felt a terrible chill as she stood on the shore. Something was wrong. A horrible feeling of loneliness washed over her. She hadn't felt that alone since her sisters had died so many lifetimes earlier. She almost wanted to call out to the odd sisters to see if they were still lurking behind the mirrors, but something told her they weren't. She didn't have to take the mirror out of her pocket. She didn't have to call them in vain. *They're gone.* She could feel it.

They're really gone. They've left me alone.

She heard her mother's words echoing in her ears again. *You are destined to be alone.*

Gothel sighed. She was waiting for the ruffians

to do their work, waiting until it was time to call out to her flower, save her from the terrible beastly men, and from the young man who had used and betrayed her. She had arranged a grand spectacle. All for Rapunzel. A ruse. And she was sure it would bring her flower back to her, back where she belonged.

Hades! I forgot the sleeping potion! Never mind. She would bring her flower back to the tower and give her the sleeping potion there, then take her to the country house herself. She didn't need Lucinda, Ruby, and Martha. Nothing else mattered but the flower. The flower and her sisters. Her real sisters. She wouldn't be alone for long.

I'll be with you soon, Sisters.

Finally, it was time. Time for the performance of her life. Time to make the commotion. Gothel would be the savior, the doting mother who saved her dear sweet daughter from the nasty thieves who played with her emotions.

Gothel called out from the darkness. "Rapunzel?"

"Mother?"

"Oh! My precious girl!"

"Mother!"

"Are you all right? Are you hurt?"

"Mother, how did you . . ."

"I was so worried about you, dear. So I followed you, and I saw them attack you, and . . . Oh my, let's go—let's go before they come to!"

Rapunzel watched Eugene sail away on his boat. Gothel could see her flower was heartbroken. She believed Eugene had betrayed her and that the only person in the world who really loved her was her mother, who was waiting for her with open arms. Rapunzel melted into a heap of tears and cried in her mother's embrace. "You were right, Mother. You were right about everything."

"I know, darling, I know."

CHAPTER XXXVII

THERE, IT NEVER HAPPENED

"Now, wash up for dinner. I'm making hazelnut soup!" Rapunzel was back in her room, at home with her mother. Heartbroken. Her mother was acting like it was just any other day. It wasn't. Rapunzel had thought she was going to have a life. A real life! But she was trapped in the tower again, never to leave, never to love. Her mother was right: the world was a horrible place.

"I really did try, Rapunzel. I tried to warn you what was out there. The world is dark, selfish, and cruel. If it finds even the slightest ray of sunshine, it destroys it."

Like my sisters, Gothel thought.

Rapunzel opened her clenched fist. She had been holding on to one of the purple flags from the celebration. On it was a golden sun, just like the sun on the King's and Queen's clothing in the mural. Just like the suns in the murals she had painted on her bedroom ceiling. Everywhere she looked there were suns and more suns.

Then it hit her. She fell backward into her vanity. In that moment, she knew. In that moment, it all made sense.

She was the lost princess.

"Rapunzel? Rapunzel, what's going on up there? Rapunzel, are you all right?" said Gothel, walking up the stairs to see what the commotion was.

Rapunzel was in shock. She stood on the landing, just looking at Gothel, seeing her for the foul woman she was. "I'm the lost princess."

"Please speak up, Rapunzel. You know how I hate the mumbling."

"I am the lost princess. Aren't I?" Rapunzel gave Gothel a wrathful look and continued. "Did

I mumble, Mother? Or should I even call you that?"

"Oh, Rapunzel, do you even hear yourself? Why would you ask such a ridiculous question?"

"It was you! It was always you."

"Everything I did was to protect you." *My flower.*

Rapunzel shoved Gothel and ran past her down the stairs. "Rapunzel!"

"I spent my entire life hiding from people who would use me for my powers," said Rapunzel, walking away from her mother.

"Rapunzel!" called Gothel, going after her.

"And all this time I should have been hiding from you!" Gothel couldn't believe how angry Rapunzel was.

"Where will you go? He won't be there for you!" said Gothel, desperate to keep her flower.

"What did you do to him?"

"That criminal will be hanged for his crimes."

"No."

"Now, now, it's all right. Listen to Mommy, all of this is as it should be." She reached to touch

Rapunzel's hair, but Rapunzel snatched her mother's hand in hers, and then she saw it. Her mother's hand was like a claw. Like a witch's hand.

"No, you were wrong about the world. And you were wrong about me. And I will never let you use my hair again," Rapunzel shouted, pushing Gothel backward into a mirror, smashing it.

"You want me to be the bad guy? Fine, now I'm the bad guy." Gothel slapped Rapunzel across the face, knocking her to the floor. "Is this what you want?"

"Mother! No!"

"I'm not your mother, remember! I'm just the witch who stole you from your real family!"

"Please! Please don't hurt me!"

"I wouldn't hurt you, dear! You think you know my story. You have it all written in your mind! You know nothing of my life, Rapunzel, or why I've made the choices I have." She put her knife to Rapunzel's throat as she chained her up.

"Rapunzel! Rapunzel, let down your hair." It was Flynn Rider. He was calling from outside.

"How . . . Never mind," said Gothel. "Now listen to me, my little flower, do as I say or I will gut that dreamboat of yours, do you understand?" She tossed Rapunzel's hair out the window for Flynn Rider to climb up.

"Do you understand?" asked Gothel.

"Yes," said Rapunzel.

"Yes, what?"

"Yes, Mother."

"That's right," Gothel said as she gagged the lost princess.

Gothel stood at the window, waiting for Flynn Rider to come in. Rapunzel was frozen in fear. She didn't know what her mother—what Gothel— would do next.

"Rapunzel, I never thought I would see you again!"

Before he could say anything else, Gothel stabbed him. She had killed before but nothing so intimate as this, and she had a keen sense of satisfaction, feeling the blade slip into his flesh and his warm blood pouring onto her hand. Rapunzel screamed through her gag, trying to reach Eugene, but the ropes kept her in place.

"Now look what you've done, Rapunzel!" Gothel said. "Oh, don't worry, dear. Our secret will die with him."

Rapunzel was terrified. Eugene was bleeding to death.

"And as for us . . . we are going where no one will ever find you again!" *We will go to the dead woods, and I will claim my place as queen once again, and I will have my sisters at my side!*

Rapunzel was struggling against her mother as Gothel tried to drag her down the secret passageway.

"Rapunzel, really! Stop already! Stop fighting me!"

"No! I won't stop! For every minute for the rest of my life, I will fight. I will never stop trying to get away from you, but if you let me save him, I will go with you."

"No, no, Rapunzel," Eugene said.

"I will never run, I will never try to escape. Just let me heal him. And you and I will be together forever. Like you want. Everything will be the way it was. I promise. Just like you want. Just let me heal him."

Together. Forever. The words were like knives in Gothel's heart. *Sisters. Together. Forever.*

Gothel agreed. She finally had her flower. Rapunzel would go without a struggle. Gothel would take her to the dead woods, and they would be together, along with her sisters. They would never grow old and they would never die. They would never turn to dust like their mother. She would never suffer the indignity of death—of the horrible death she had given her mother. She was finally going to have the life she wanted.

"Eugene! Oh, I'm so sorry! Everything is going to be okay, though. I promise. You have to trust me, come on."

"I can't let you do this!"

He was dying, and Rapunzel's heart was breaking as she watched him slipping away from her. "And I can't let you die," Rapunzel told him.

"But if you do this, then you will die." She

knew Eugene was right, but there was no choice. "Hey, it's going to be all right." She didn't know who she was trying to convince—Eugene or herself.

"Rapunzel, wait," he said as he touched the side of her face. And before she could stop him, he sliced off her hair with a piece of broken mirror.

"Eugene, what—?" She held her hair in her hands as she watched it die and turn brown. It looked like dead leaves.

"No!" Gothel screamed as she tried to gather the dying hair to her. "No, no, no! What have you done?" And then it was happening. She was suffering the same fate as her mother. She started to wither. She started to age. It was horrific. And the pain, it was worse than she had imagined. It consumed her. It devoured her from within. "What have you done?" She ran to the mirror, trying to find the odd sisters, trying to find someone who could help her. She couldn't leave her sisters alone. What would become of them? She had failed them. She had failed her sisters. She was going to die. *I can't leave my sisters! I can't!* She screamed as the pain filled her body. There was no escaping it. Had her mother felt that way when she died? Had it been that horrendous for her? Gothel was turning to dust. She could feel herself falling away. And she saw Rapunzel's horrified face as Gothel tripped and fell out the window. The last thing she saw was the last thing her mother had seen.

A look of utter revulsion and horror.

EPILOGUE

Circe put down the book of fairy tales and sighed. "He died."

Snow dropped the teacup she had been holding. Her sweet face crumpled into tears. She didn't know what to say. "I'm sorry I broke your teacup," she said, looking down at the pieces.

"Eugene died in Rapunzel's arms, Snow."

Snow cried even harder "It's not fair."

"No, it's not!" Circe walked over to one of her sisters' large mirrors she had propped up against one of the onyx ravens that flanked the fireplace. "Show me Rapunzel." She saw Rapunzel crying over Eugene's body. Circe closed her eyes, placed her hand on the mirror, and said the words:

Epilogue

Flower, gleam and glow
Let her power shine
Make the clock reverse
Bring back what once was hers

Heal what has been hurt
Change the fates' design
Save what has been lost
Bring back what once was hers

What once was hers

As Rapunzel's tears fell, they created spiraling golden light that grew and twisted around them like wild creeping vines dancing around the tower, and from the vines blossomed a beautiful golden flower.

"Did you do that?" asked Snow as she watched Eugene come back to life.

"I'm not sure," Circe said. "Rapunzel may have had a bit of the flower still within her."

Snow smiled at her cousin. "Either way she has her happy ending."

"She does," said Circe, frowning.

"What's wrong, Circe?"

"I . . . I'm not the real Circe."

"Of course you're real, Circe. I promise you. You're very real." Snow rushed to Circe, took her into her arms, and kissed her again and again. "Listen to me, Cousin. You're the bravest, most loving woman I have ever met. You are real. And I love you. Don't ever let me hear you thinking differently. Don't ever think you are less." The house started to rumble and shake, shifting and moving rapidly. "What's happening?"

This time the ladies didn't panic. This time they simply went to the window and saw the endless black sea, streaked with light and glittering with stars, transmute, swirling and morphing and somehow connecting to the world they knew, until the celestial world they had been living in was entirely gone and they were once again in the many kingdoms.

"Circe! We're home!" said Snow White, her face filled with happiness.

Circe smiled back at her sweet cousin. She could tell Snow wasn't ready to return to her old life. She wanted more adventure. She wanted to see more of the world. "Should we go see Rapunzel's wedding on our way to Morningstar?" she asked, hoping Snow would say yes.

"Are they getting married already?" asked Snow, laughing to herself.

"No, not for a few years yet. But I can take us there," said Circe.

Snow White laughed again. "Yes! Let's see her happy with her family. I would love that!"

"So would I! And will you come with me to check on Mrs. Tiddlebottom?" asked Circe, remembering the poor woman left alone in her country house.

"Oh yes, of course! I almost forgot about her!" Snow said, also remembering Gothel's sisters and wondering what Circe was planning to do about them. "And I will go with you to Morningstar afterwards to check on Nanny and Tulip," she added.

"Thank you so much, Snow. I honestly don't know what I would do without you."

"I love you, Circe. We're in this together. I promise."

"Good, because I think I'm going to need you in the days to come."

"What's wrong, Circe?"

"I'm not sure. I won't know until I read the journals my mothers wrote during their time in the dead woods with Gothel."

Snow White wanted nothing more than to see her cousin happy. But she knew in her soul that if Circe let her sisters out of the dreamscape, she would never have peace. She would never have happiness.

"Are you going to let your mothers use the mirrors now that the story is over?"

"No. Let them sit in darkness. Let them wonder. I'm done with them."

THE END